WHY WON'T MY HUSBAND WORK?

||| | ||||||||||| ||| | |||||| ||||
I0543166

The Struggle Is ......

Us/Them Series

Authored by Tori T.

Cover Art by Ghislain Viau

A fictitious novel. All names, characters, workplaces, and occurrences are totally fictitious and of the author's imagination. Inspired by conversation and girl talk but does not resemble any actual events, or persons, and if so it's coincidental.

ISBN - 978-0-9965275-1-4

ISBN: -10:09965275-1-6

Library of Congress Control/Case Number: 1-2359540989

Harr-Lilt Publishing

est. 2014

Printed in the United States

DEDICATION ◈

Dedicated to my best friend, Aulbry Taylor,

who said write and keep writing.

Dedicated to two very special young ladies,

Ms. D. B. and Ms. T. I.

who said, "Go for it!" Through our funny conversations

and what if's, this book came to life.

And! For all the women whose circumstances are similar,

your words

are in print and may enable you to put your lives into

perspective.

CONTENTS

INTRODUCTION: THE STRUGGLE IS REAL! ◈

Seven professional women at LEKO Aeronautics, the sole breadwinners in their households, deal with raising their non-working husbands along with their children. Believing they were married to the men of their dreams, their lives had turned into a gamut of empty promises, nights of bloodshed tears, and a curriculum of *Enabling*. These men made promises that had remained only promises and were yet to be fulfilled. These women wondered how they all ended up working in the same place with the same problem, "Their husbands refused to work."

Unbeknown to them, Ms. Lindy, was picking up the pieces, and restoring their husband's souls. Ms. Lindy was a 36-year-old self-proclaimed, unlicensed sex and marriage therapist, who believed that she was keeping their marriages together. She was trying to keep these men at home with their families, but for a price.

Ba'Mynn Hartford at 38 years old was a beautiful young woman, and as the years flew by, she grew even more beautiful. Born of French and African parentage, she had been sheltered, pampered, and treated like a princess. Standing at five foot five and smart as a whip, she had been the pride and joy of her parents.

At seventeen years of age, and after only one night, Ba'Mynn had found herself pregnant and unmarried. As a result, she had been forced out of her parent's home because of her delicate, but unwed condition. To make matters worse, her parents believed Ba'Mynn would never live this down and her life would be ruined.

Kristen "Krissy" Windsor, was 33 years old and had been married to the supposedly man of her dreams for nine years, but was seriously considering walking away. Not quite beautiful, but pretty enough to warrant a second look, she had met Karl. Karl was a smooth talker, had worked for the IRS when they met, but quit shortly after they were married.

During a *friend's night out* together, Karl had poured it on thick. The first time they met, this man had informed her that he would marry her within the year. After promising her the world, Krissy began to date him. Again, their mutual friends warned her that he didn't like to work, had a son he didn't support, and was just too emotional. Some had even said he was a stalker and too clingy. After dating for six months, Krissy saw only the perfect man. Feeling happy and satisfied, she had ignored her jealous friends, and married him anyway. She had walked in with her eyes wide open. At 23 years of age, she became his wife, and that was the only promise he had ever made good on.

Dawn Garrett was a 46-year-old professional married woman with two adult daughters, one adult son, and a husband with a wounded soul. Dawn stood five feet seven inches tall, and was slightly heavier than she would have liked. Graced with a full head of beautiful bright red hair (though it was unruly and untamed most of the time), it was layered against her pale white skin. Not very pretty, Dawn was borderline homely, but makeup did change things for her.

Consumed with loneliness after the death of her first husband she wanted, No! She needed someone in her life. She had married Bence as soon as he'd stepped off the immigration train. You see, Bence had entered the country illegally from Europe, and was unable to work a regular job, because he had no green card. "He has no self-confidence so I have to help him. I'm going to get a second job, because I love him. My youngest daughter, Belle, is my headache. She's truly beautiful, but has always had too many emotions."

Priza Oliveira was a 42-year-old professional, who supported her husband, and their two children (his biological children that she had adopted). "I'm working two jobs so my husband can finish school, but he's not in school, and stays home everyday." Priza was a manager at one place and an online professor at the local university. Her husband had not worked in over two years, was losing weight, and not sleeping. "I wonder if he's sick, OMG! Maybe he has HIV/Aids or something." Combing her sleek brown hair to the back (which fell in a naturally wavy pattern), she looked in the mirror at her piercing green eyes, and liked what she saw. After all of these years, she still had the confidence she needed to excel in her professional life, but unfortunately lacked it in her personal life. Eirik had quit working two years ago, and was supposed to go back to college to get a better paying job. She had looked forward to staying home with the children, and was still waiting.

Alexandria "Alex" Stottler was a married 40-year-old professional and mother of two who believed in her husband. Not the average looking mother, Alexandria was naturally beautiful and exhibited the grace and body of a fashion model. Born in the Chicago housing projects, she had acquired an academic scholarship with a full ride to one of the top colleges in the country. During college, she had modeled to earn extra money and made quite a name for herself.

Alexandria's husband, Max, was a starving artist, and from the looks of it he would always be starving. The paintings were becoming scarce, and so were his earnings. Max was waiting to be discovered. In the beginning, his paintings had made enough income to assist with the household expenses, but now it wasn't enough to depend upon. He'd made so many promises, but none had manifested. "He said he would take care of me, but it's been fourteen years, and I'm still waiting. I can't leave him because he's the father of my children. God gave me this husband and I have to make it work. I have to make it work, because I need him. I mean he needs me and the children needs him. Honestly, I don't know what I mean anymore."

Gabrielle "Gabby" Hough was a beautiful 22-year-old strawberry blonde haired girl with icy blue eyes, who'd been married less than a year. She and her husband, Reese, had graduated from college together. They had made big plans and had dreams prior to the accident. "I know he will get a job soon, but right now he's disabled. In the meantime, I'm working very hard to support our household."

"I may be pregnant, but I haven't confirmed it yet. My doctor advised me to come in, but I'm too busy. But wait! I can't take off from work for medical misfortunes. I have to work, because he doesn't. Otherwise, it would be two non-working mugs having a baby."

Looking pitiful she kept talking, "My parents are angry because I got married against their wishes. They wanted me to wait until I was older, financially stable, and established. Although I graduated from college, I have an entry-level professional position that's in jeopardy, because I'm always late due to my early morning duties."

Elissa Langston was a 35 year married professional. At 5'10, she was a lovely woman. Reared in a loving and well-educated family, she was very mild mannered and nurturing. If her family knew about her living situation, they would drag her home by her hair. Fortunately, she kept them at arm's length, and was thankful they lived in another country.

"I have been married for over seven years, and my husband Patrick has never worked. Patrick is a professional student and is overly educated.

Our first year of marriage, he completed a medical assistant course. Years two and three, he spent completing a two-year degree. Years four and five, he completed his Bachelor's Degree in Journalism. Year six, he attended an online university and obtained a Master's Degree in Journalism, but still has no fricking job. Hooray! Year seven, Monday through Saturday, he spends time at his male friend's nail shop. Oh! Did I tell you? He plans to be part owner at this nail salon. *Get Nailed* No! It's not funny. No fricking kidding! It's called *Get Nailed*. Blockbuster Time! The rest of his time is spent watching talk show reruns and the host."

Elissa was seriously considering walking away.

1 PRIZA, "HE SAID HE WAS GOING TO SCHOOL" ◆

Lying on her therapist' sofa, with the back of her hand shielding her eyes, Priza breathed heavily and began her session. She thought about what Eirik had promised almost two years ago. "Priza, I'm going to resign my position and finish my graduate degree, so I can get a better job. The problem is, I can't work and go to school at the same time. After I graduate, you won't have to work anymore. You can stay home with our children, teach, and be my wife." She had welcomed the idea and supported his plan.

"Dr. T, he has broken every single one of his promises. Although, I remind him every semester, Eirik still hasn't enrolled in any classes. Not only is he not attending school, this man is not working. The house is always a mess, and when I get home from work, the kids still need help with their homework. He plays video games all day, and he never cooks dinner. To top it off, he doesn't seem to care one way or the other. Dr. T., why won't my husband go back to work? I'm starting to wonder if something is wrong with me for putting up with it."

Peering at Priza over her glasses, Dr. T. provided insight, "Priza, up until a year ago things were going well for the two of you. I thought having the children in your home, would be a positive influence in your marriage. Things have changed and you're not happy. If mamma isn't happy, AIN'T nobody going to be happy. I have some homework for you. I want you to answer these questions." Dr. T. gave Priza the paperwork and ordered, "Answer all of these questions and I will see you on Monday. Pick his brain and find out what is going on? There is a piece missing from this puzzle and it's up to you to find out what it is. Caution! (Dr. T waved her finger) Tread slowly, because it could become dangerous to the marriage. Don't make him feel threatened." Dr. T. stood up, signaling the end of the session.

Still seated, Priza kept talking, "You know, I never thought about all of this stuff before. I have never held him accountable as far as what bills he was paying. I just labeled it as household expenses. He has been looking ill lately, and has cut off all of his hair. It's as if he's living for the moment. You have given me a lot to think about. Thank you, Dr. T." Priza stood up quietly and walked out the door and into the parking garage. She got into her truck, drove onto the expressway, and headed home. Totally forgetting to tread slowly, Priza declared! "Today is the day. I'm going to make a stand."

Steering her car into the local Home Depot parking lot, Priza parked her mechanically equipped Escalade and walked into the store. As she walked toward the hardware department, a salesperson, a very young salesperson at that, approached her.

He walked up and spoke to her, "Hello ma'am is there something I can help you find?"

Leaning heavily onto her prosthetic legs and attempting to disguise her disability, Priza looked at his nametag and answered, "Dominique! Yes, you can. I'm changing the door locks at my house and I would like the best you have."

Assessing her beauty, Dominique answered, "Yes pretty, I mean please follow me over to aisle seventeen and I will show you what we have."

Walking behind Dominique, Priza stared *Cougarishly* at his physique and showed a subtle appreciation for his nice firm frame. "I will need two sets of locks for my front and back doors, and I would really like something strong and sturdy."

"Yes ma'am right away," said Dominique as he stopped in the middle of aisle seventeen. "Okay! Here we have the King Master's Power Lockset; it has proven to be strong, solid, and enduring. In addition, it has a warranty of 15 years, and it only cost $24.99. We also have the Freedom Keeper's Lockset which is our top of the line brand and it sells for $49.99, and it comes with a lifetime warranty." As, Dominique continued to talk about the quality of the locks; Priza found herself drifting into the past while contemplating the future.

Priza daydreamed and wondered what it would have been like, if she had married a man who delivered on his promises. She also wondered what her life would have been like if she was different. After all, Eirik had pleaded with her to allow him to take time off so he could go back to school and finish his college degree. Yes, she had agreed, because he had made it sound so good. She had envisioned being a stay at home mom, and sharing those special moments with their children. That was almost two years ago and he had not taken one class, and she was still the sole provider for the family. She finished her degree, went to work as a manager in an aeronautical firm, and had been taking care of him and their responsibilities ever since.

In fact, right now she was working two jobs so they could take the family trips the kids had grown to love every summer. She also paid private school tuition to ensure they had the right education, and all of the opportunities she'd been given as a child. If her parents were alive to see this, they would have initiated an intervention to ensure her mental state was intact. They had long since passed away from a tragic car crash and left Priza without any siblings. Although she had other relatives, sometime she felt so alone in the world.

Born in the late seventies and without her lower limbs, Priza's mother and father had never allowed her to feel sorry for herself. Her parents had always encouraged, supported, and demanded she live up to her full potential. Never finding time to feel sorry for herself, she was allowed to explore life for what it was and what it could be. Always showered with love and being the only child, she felt as if she could conquer the world.

A very young Priza would drag herself across the floor and play with her dog, Monet. At the age of three, she was fitted with prosthetic legs, and had never slowed down. She would scurry after Monet until playing with her became monotonous. In fact, she was the one, at the age of seven, who demanded to carry Monet into the vet's office when she had to be put down.

She had been one of the most popular girls all through school. Although she never wore dresses to school, she was always stylishly clad because she was her mother's daughter. Only close friends and school officials knew the full range of her disability. Voted class valedictorian for her senior class, Priza wore a dress to school for the very first time at her graduation.

Priza received overwhelming and heartwarming applause during her high school graduation, and knew that the world would be hers. Having decided to go to college, she felt as if she could do anything and everything this world had to offer. After spending a very active and fun summer with her friends, Priza was ready to go off to college.

While riding her scooter around Lankon University, she had met Mr. Eirik Halldor, Mr. Married Eirik Halldor. His name meant "Ever ruler" and "Rock." I mean hell! How much more solid could he get. She had been intrigued by his good looks, and his diligence about life. Although interested, she remembered he was married, and had kept her distance. She learned he was from Brazil, and coincidentally, she would be visiting Brazil in a couple of years. Maybe, just maybe, she would run into him and meet his family. Lankon University was also where she met her BFF, Alexandria, and they had become inseparable, and was still inseparable. Alexandria was her family, and their children went to the same private school.

Two years later, Priza was reacquainted with Eirik while in Brazil, with her college friends. She had run into him at one of the local beach. Newly divorced, Eirik was considering moving to the United States with his mother, but hesitated about leaving his children behind.

In spite of, Eirik and Priza had instantly fell in love, and had gotten married, all within six months. They were married in Brazil, but made their home back in the United States. Eirik's mother Kate had followed with her own move, to be near her only child. Eirik frequently traveled back and forth to see his children, and Priza supported his traveling. She had met his children and their mother, and genuinely liked and cared about them all.

"Uh ma'am, which lock are you interested in?" Priza quickly looked up and Dominique was holding a set of locks in each hand.

"Freedom, huh!" Standing tall and with finality, "I will take two sets of the Freedom Keeper's locksets, thank you." After purchasing the locks, Priza stood up straight, walked out of the store, got into her truck, and drove off.

Several minutes later, she pulled into her driveway, and was barely able to see as the tears rolled down her cheeks. She parked the Escalade and quietly gathered her purse and belongings. Grabbing for the door handle, she hesitated and sat quietly. She looked at the door locks, and decided, today was really the day she would give Eirik his eviction notice. Eirik's time was up, "GET OUT!" Priza shouted! "GET OUT!" and startled herself. She put her head down on the steering wheel, still crying as she reflected on the past few years of her life.

Calmly sobbing she thought, "What did I do to deserve this? Surely God would not let me continue to live and suffer like this. I have survived many obstacles before, but this is too much. Hell, I was born without legs, but I've managed to live a productive life. Am I not an influential contributor to this society? Am I! I mean haven't I!" Priza screamed, and pounded the steering wheel. Finally pulling herself together, she reapplied her makeup, grabbed her purse, and exited her truck.

Priza put on her happy face before entering her

home, that she alone was paying for, and demanded self-courage. She turned the doorknob and walked into the house. "Hi, I'm home." With no answer, she walked through the foyer and into the family room nearly tripping over the toys on the floor. She thought, "I have asked them so many times before to please clean up their toys when they were not playing with them. Priza was referring to her ten-year-old son; Sergio and her seven-year-old daughter; Niema, Eirik's children from his first marriage. The children had lived in Brazil with their mother until she had unexpectedly passed away from a heart attack.

With sincere fear of losing her children, their mother, Leanna, had never allowed them out of Brazil. Sadly, after a couple of years, their mother had passed away and Priza became a new mother. Thinking she would never have children, they had become her life along with Eirik, and she loved them as her own.

Sitting on the sofa playing video games were her son, daughter, and Eirik. Looking up with the game controller in his hands, "Hey Babe! How was your day?" Standing, he walked over and kissed Priza on her cheek, as Priza turned her head away. She had immediately froze and turned toward the children. Puzzled, Eirik scratched his head, and stared at his wife.

"So what's for dinner, you three?" Priza stepped around her husband to gather up the scattered toys and clutter around the floor.

Eirik continued scratching his head and became defensive, "You must've had a bad day because your welcome wasn't very nice. Dinner huh! I left a message on your voicemail asking you to stop and pick up something for dinner. I'm tired today. I drove the kids to school and I picked them up. I don't even have any clean socks or underwear. Did you do the laundry? What about that?"

Priza couldn't believe what she was hearing. With tears running down her cheeks and her back to them, she mumbled, "Sergio, Niema, please go to your room while I get dinner ready." Without a word, the children stood up and walked toward the stairs. Priza always felt bad when the children witnessed their negative exchanges. She feared they would interpret it, as they would have to leave and wouldn't have a mother anymore.

Sergio whispered to Niema, "They are going to fight again. Dad didn't cook, clean, or do laundry."

"I'm scared Sergio, I think mommy is going to get a divorce. Dad spent the day with grandma again, and mommy's mad." Niema had been almost four when her mother died, and loved Priza as her mother.

"Of course they're not getting a divorce, because everyone argues. Besides women always do the cooking and cleaning when they get home from work."

Looking puzzled, Niema asks, "But shouldn't daddy help mommy? And, why doesn't daddy work like mommy?"

Shrugging his shoulders, "Niema, you have a lot to learn." Sergio grabbed Niema's hand and continued up the stairs in silence. Priza was busy cleaning the kitchen while the salmon sat on the countertop, frozen.

Eirik followed her into the kitchen and commented, "Look I left you a message to pick up dinner, but you never responded. I'm trying to keep us on the right track. I mean, what do you want from me?"

With her back to Eirik, she struggled to open the handle-less dishwasher, in which Eirik had promised to repair for the past four months, but hadn't. "RIGHT TRACK! Talking about right track. Did you register for classes today?" Turning around and staring at him, she noticed his lost weight and dark circles beneath his eyes. Not wanting to appear empathetic, she stood firm.

Eirik sighed deeply and replying defensively, "I called the admission's office last week, and I told you they weren't accepting new students until the spring semester. You know all of this because I told you last week. All you do is nag. Nag! Nag! I'm sick of this and I'm sick of you! I work hard around this house and I take care of our kids. I also went over to my mother's house because I had to fix her kitchen sink."

Priza turned around and slammed the salmon into the sink, "Eirik almost two years ago you stopped working so you could return to school, while the kids attended school during the day. We agreed that you would take time to complete your degree, while being accessible to Niema. You were to transport Niema back and forth to school and get Sergio on the bus. I drive Niema to school almost everyday, and drop Sergio off most of the time. You have not taken one class, and the house is always a mess. I help Niema and Sergio with their homework every evening when I get home from work, and you continue to do nothing." Shaking with tears rolling down her cheeks, Priza yelled! "Yes, sometimes you take the kids to school, but the house is always filthy, the laundry is undone, and there is never any dinner prepared when I get home. None of this makes sense. I work sixty hours every week, and that excludes commuting back and forth. You sit on your butt all day, play video games, and talk privately on your cell phones into the wee hours. Things are broken here, but you leave and go to your mother's house to fix things. Is there anything going on I should know about, because none of this makes sense? Eirik, are you cheating?"

Surprised by her outburst, Eirik cowered, "Priza, I love you and you are everything to me. I would never look at another woman." Pleading he continued, "I'm doing the best that I can. Tomorrow, I promise I will cook dinner, wash the laundry, and transport the kids. I will go down to the college campus, and speak to an advisor."

Priza noticed that Eirik was trembling, and wondered if he was feeling well. She also noticed he had shaved his hair off. Pushing that thought out of her head, she knew she had to keep pushing. "I've heard all of this before. Tomorrow, not next week, not next month, I would like you to go to the college, find a job, or make other living arrangements. Eirik, you have two weeks to make some changes or you have to go. I'm sick of this crap and I'm SICK OF YOU!" The nerve of him saying he was sick of her. Priza reached into her purse and pulled out the bag of locksets. "If you don't register for classes or return to work, I will change the locks and you will have to move out. Better yet, move in with your mother, you spend most days there anyway."

Eirik was trembling, and short of breath, but managed to speak, "Wait a minute! I said I love you and this is my house too. What do you want from me? This is OUR home, and I provided half the down payment."

Staring at him with swollen eyes, Priza screamed, "I want you to be the husband and the father you promised to be. For our entire marriage, and even before the children came to live with us, you haven't been fulfilling your obligations to me or the household. As soon as we closed on this house, you decreased your work hours. Furthermore, you have worked a total of three years combined our entire marriage. I make the monthly mortgage payments. You have two weeks to make some progress, or I will take the kids and leave."

Sighing again, Eirik replied, "Firstly, I won't

allow you to take my children because they belong to me. Secondly, I will show you I'm serious. I'm going to show you I'm serious about completing my degree. You just wait and see."

Taken aback by his words, Priza charged! "Oh! So they are your kids. Okay, so take care of them."

Finished with dinner, Priza showered and dressed Niema, kissed Sergio good night, and went to bed. (Sighing and lying down she realized it was well after midnight.) Almost immediately, she had fallen asleep with tears on her cheeks.

Five hours later, the alarm clock was ringing. She reached over and saw it was already 5:30 a.m. Having to commute an hour to get to work by 08:00 a.m. was taking its toll on her. Yawning softly, Priza reached over to touch Eirik and realized he wasn't there. Seeing the light underneath the bedroom door, Priza reached for her legs, strapped them on, slowly got up, and went downstairs. Seated on the sofa was Eirik, playing video games and talking on his cellphone.

Staring at him she replied, "My thoughts exactly," and she turned and went back upstairs.

2 KRISSY, "EVICTED AGAIN!" •

Krissy had been extremely pretty, almost
beautiful on her wedding day. Her jet-black hair had
flowed down her back, and complimented her creamy
skin. Her beautiful ivory gown clung to her 105-
pound figure. Her parents had sponsored both her
wedding and honeymoon, and loved how Karl treated
their daughter. In the beginning, they had cared very
deeply for him, that is, until they started to notice the
negative things about him.

Unfortunately, there was another side to Karl
that Krissy didn't share with anyone. In fact, Karl
was extremely emotional. After two years of
marriage, and the arrival of their daughter Hannah,
Karl had quit his job. Another year passed, and Karl
had overdosed on a bottle of pills. She rushed him to

the emergency room, and they pumped his stomach. With Hannah in tow, Krissy had sat at his bedside daily. He had refused to talk to her and just stared at the wall.

Immediately afterwards, Karl spent several weeks in the psychiatric ward, and later came home in a better place. But he still didn't return to work. Afraid of anyone finding out, Krissy hid this part of her life, and told people he was away on a business trip. The only positive thing she had gotten out of this marriage was her beautiful daughter, Hannah. She had also been graced with the *gift of moving* several times in a year, and all because her husband refused to work.

Krissy was sitting at her desk when she noticed Priza, and placed her phone on hold. Grabbing Priza's shirttail, Krissy spoke with desperation, "Please, I need to talk to you. I'm desperate and I need help. My life is a mess. Please!"

Heaving a sigh, Priza yawned from the lack of sleep, and quickly looked around to make sure the coast was clear. Carefully lowering herself to prevent unsnapping her prosthetics, she kneeled beside Krissy in the cubicle, and reluctantly listened to Krissy's problems.

Krissy began to speak with tears rolling down her cheeks, "We just got evicted, again and Karl isn't working, again! Apparently, he spent the rent money, but I don't know what he spent it on. My daughter is upset because she has to leave her new school and friends, again! Hannah is only seven years old and we have moved eleven times since she was born. My parents are angry and want me to move home with them. I don't want to leave my husband, and I refuse to borrow any more money."

Krissy paused briefly, "When I left this morning, he said he was going to the employment agency to pick up some temporary work. I just called him and he informed me that he stayeed home for the day. Do you know what he said? He said, "I was only going to make a few dollars anyway. I don't like working for those places because they hire too many criminals. The way he said it was so condescending and disrespectful. I told him, something is always better than zero and we could've used it for food, gas, or something else. I responded by hanging up in his face." Krissy placed her head on the desk, unaware that her phone had reverted to ready. "Hello! Hello! Hello! Hello!" sounded from the telephone console.

Priza realizing that Krissy was active pointed to her green light, and stood up. "Kris, we can't talk here, because you will be overheard and we don't want to get fired. Seriously, I have my own problems, and could be a single parent before the end of this month. Look, let's talk about this at break time in the *Quiet Room*."

Krissy sat up, regained her composure, and whispered, "Okay, thanks Priza. I'm sorry to unload on you this morning, but I needed to talk to someone. I will meet you in the *Quiet Room*, and I appreciate you listening to me rant. I'm just tired of his refusing to work, and not handling his responsibilities. I'm sick and tired of being sick and tired."

After informing Krissy to contact the Employee Assistance Services (EAS), Priza hugged her and walked back to her office. It was very uncomfortable listening to Krissy speak about her husband in that way. Priza mumbled to herself, "I can't get involved with her stuff, because I have my own stuff. What can I say? He's a loser and she should get rid of him. At least my husband has some college behind him and will be going back to school shortly. But who was he talking to at five-thirty in the morning?" Priza reconnected her phone line. "Good morning, welcome to LEKO Aeronautics, how can I help you today?"

An hour later, Krissy sent Priza an email with the words "break time," and logged out her computer. Turning around slowly, she mouthed to her team leader, "Lish, I'm going on my fifteen minute break." Affirming Lish's permission, Krissy looked over, made eye contact with Priza, and started toward the *Quiet Room*.

Priza finished her call and disconnected her telephone. While reinforcing her legs straps, she wondered how to support to Krissy, without becoming overly involved. She herself was running on fumes from the lack of sleep, and was struggling to get though the day. Priza took the long route around the building, before arriving at the *Quiet Room*. Standing at the door, she straightened her back and thought, "After all her situation is much worse than mine."

Krissy sat by the bay window and observed as Priza walked toward her with almost a limp. Her gait was nearly mechanical. Priza reached the bay window seat and sat down next to her. Krissy had never noticed the limp before and hesitated before speaking. She almost felt guilty for pouring on her problems, and her voice trembled as she spoke, "Thank you Priza. Thank you for talking to me, because I don't know what to do."

Priza sensed her desperation, and felt she had to

offer something. "How long has this been going on? Was he like this before you married him? I mean you had to have some signs, some kind of inkling of what he was like."

Krissy felt uncomfortable, and spoke with her head down, "He was so wonderful at first. Then, I started to notice little things. He started to make promises and he didn't keep them. He called off from work too often. When we got married, he worked for the Internal Revenue Service (IRS), and his income was steady. With the arrival of our daughter, Hannah, he got worse. Everytime I questioned him, he became explosive and verbally abusive. He has never raised a hand to me, but his words cut through me like a knife." Krissy took a breath, and kept talking.

"He hasn't worked a regular job in a long time,

and my parents are angry because we are moving again. The last time we stayed with them, he had a big fight with my dad, and was kicked out of their house. My dad questioned his sanity and stability, and he tore up my dad's man cave."

Krissy paused long enough to take a sip of water, "My parents said Hannah and I could stay, but Karl wasn't welcome anymore. I couldn't leave him, so we left and stayed in a seedy motel until I could save enough to rent a place. Last week, the mortgage company called me, and we are three months behind. I've been waiting for him to say something, but he has said nothing. If evicted, we may have to move back in with them. Not to mention, we have stayed with them over five times throughout this marriage, and my dad says Karl is never welcome again. In addition, I have been paying his child support from his first marriage for two years."

In silence, Krissy waited for Priza's response. Sensing she should say something Krissy continued, "The IRS garnished my wages for his back child support, and took all of my income tax refund. His response was that my money was his money, so we should take care of his son."

Feeling slightly uncomfortable, she compared her own situation and realized it was way too much information. "Krissy, it's time to get back to our desks, because we still have a job to do." Before leaving, Priza placed the EAS card in her hand, and ordered! "Call them. We have to forget about home right now, and concentrate on our clients. Girl you have to pray, stay prayed up, and keep praying, and that is all I can offer. Pray and go home to your parents, at least you have an out from your situation."

Krissy listened and thought about Karl at home and wondered what he was doing.

Lindy's home was like Grand Central Station today, because her mother's therapist and caregivers were attending to her needs. She watched the caregivers shower and dress her mother, and finally put her back to bed for a nap.

Lindy spoke with the therapist, and knew that her mother had reached her full physical capacity. The therapist confirmed that the Multiple Sclerosis (MS) had completely robbed Ming of her physical freedom, and Lindy sadly acknowledged it.

Afterwards, Lindy escorted the therapist to the door, as she needed to get ready for her appointment with Karl. Walking back into her suite, she called Karl and asked, "What's your love prescription today?"

Karl was stretched out on the bed daydreaming about spending the rest of his life with Lindy. He smiled genuinely as he thought about her, "She's beautiful, she's smart, and oh what she does to me. I could spend the rest of my life with this woman."

His cell phone rang and he returned to reality. Looking at his phone, he saw it was Lindy, "Hi. Yes, I want a Geisha Girl today. Please wear a beautiful red kimono with nothing underneath, and wear your hair in the traditional fashion. I want the brightest shade of red lipstick you can find, and I want your eyelashes long and seductive. Please be clean-shaven, and drown yourself in a perfume by Versace because I like it like that. Yes, I will pay the extra hundred dollars for the last request. Okay, I will see you soon."

Lindy acknowledged Karl's instructions and relaxed. His order would be easy to fill as she and her mother often sat dressed in his requested prescription. She smiled because it was time to shave anyway, and an extra hundred dollars was always nice. Sitting at her vanity table, she began to make up her face, and thought about why she'd become a therapist. She was close to completing her doctorate degree, and would put away this profession, for good.

At 18 years of age, Lindy had went off to college, but returned home before the end of the school year. Her father passed away during her first year of college, Ming was distraught as she had loved him dearly, and Lindy was numb. At the same time, Ming had been diagnosed with MS, and had beckoned her home. She returned home, started her profession, and took over the household responsibilities.

In the beginning, Ming inquired about her work, and Lindy vaguely replied, "I'm just repairing the souls of broken individuals, while soothing their egos. If I don't feed and secure them, I mean who will. I'm not doing anything wrong, and I don't consummate the relationships." Ming was extremely embarrassed by Lindy's behavior, and decided to ignore it for the sake of peace and sanity.

Lindy had nervously smiled and continued her career of soothing other women's husbands. That's right *other women's husband.* "Besides, I'm providing a weekly service to broken souls, making up to a thousand dollars per husband, and I do get overtime. I'm averaging thousands per week plus tips, and ladies! It's your money and it's well spent. Yes, you should work a second job. Yes, you should give your husband a raise, because I need periodic pay raises for my incidentals. Besides, a girl has to protect herself. You see I'm the woman he wants you to be. Mainly, I don't complain, I provide a service and I LISTEN to them without any backlash. I'm keeping them at home with you, so you should be paying and thanking me."

Jumping, at the knock on her door, she knew it would be her mother. She loved her mother very much, but she could work one's nerve with the morality thing. Hearing another knock at the door, she hesitated before answering, "Come in." Lindy crossed her fingers that her mother wouldn't start an argument with the same annoying questions, "Where are you going?" or "Who are you going to see?"

Ming's caregiver, Mabel, rolled her wheelchair through the door. Ming looked at her daughter and wasn't very happy. "Lindy, what time will you be coming back? The caregivers would like to leave by six o'clock." Ming wondered why she was dressing up as if spending the day with her. Staring at her she thought, "Probably going somewhere to meet somebody's husband. My daughter is a total embarrassment to me. If only her father was here. This behavior wasn't tolerated in my culture."

In the beginning, Ming always wondered how they lived in such a beautiful house and her daughter paid for everything. Now that she was aware of Lindy's profession, she didn't ask many questions to avoid arguments. Fighting with Lindy drained her and they would go days without speaking. Goodness knows she loved her daughter, as she was her only child. Realizing her daughter was talking to her, she focused on what she was saying.

Lindy continued to powder her face, while

talking to Ming, "Mother, I will be home by four this evening, I won't be gone that long. We will watch a movie together, and I'll bring dinner from the sushi restaurant. I'm just spending some *me* time today and wanted to honor you by wearing this." Lindy felt bad lying to her, but had to make a living for them.

Ming was from another country, and had never worked a day in her life, so Lindy went to work. She used the skill that came natural to all women, and made a good living for them. It paid for their house, Lindy's college, Naomi (Range Rover), and most of her mother's medical care. Lindy gave Ming her father's entire pension, and Ming saved it for Lindy (Lindy wasn't aware), for after she was gone.

Not quite satisfied with her answer, but refusing to argue, Ming instructed Mabel to push her back to her suite. "Okay Mabel, I'm ready." After all, her daughter was an adult and could take care of herself.

Lindy finished dressing, waved goodbye to her mother, and went out of the garage door. She got into Naomi, and drove to her mid-week healing session. Driving, she sang along with TLC's "Scrubs," and thought about Karl and his neediness. She hoped he wouldn't start with the love stuff again. Several of her clients were becoming overly attached, and she was considering restructuring her schedule by securing new clients. In fact, she thought about it daily.

Arriving ten minutes early, she parked behind the house so nobody could see her. Stepping out of Naomi, she crept to the back of the house and knocked, "Hey Karl, it's Lindy. Karl, I'm here, open the door." She pulled out her cell phone to call him, but he quickly opened the door, and ushered her in.

Karl had forgotten about Krissy.

Seated at her desk, Krissy looked around to see if the coast was clear, and made her routine call to Karl. She dialed her home phone number and waited for his answer. Karl was supposed to take Hannah to school, and should be home alone. He didn't answer so she hung up, and wondered if he was out looking for gainful employment.

Karl had forgotten about Krissy's routine phone calls, and deliberately ignored them. Lying on his marital bed with Lindy, his five hundred dollar per week *Love Bunny*, he was feeling kind of special this morning, "Girl, you make me feel like a full grown man. Look at me! I want to cater to you." Stopping, he asked, "Are you sure, I'm the only one you are seeing? You see Lindy, I love you, and I want to see more of you." Lindy had walked in and flaunted her near perfect body in his requested outfit, and Karl had melted. He immediately loosened her hair and watched it fall to her waist. He had stripped the kimono from her body and pounced on her like a leopard. Playfully, he licked her toes until she screamed, "No more."

Lying in Krissy's bed, again Karl thought about Krissy's daily phone patrols. He quickly dismissed them, because he didn't like being policed. Krissy drummed her fingers on the desk as she spoke into her cell phone, "Karl, please answer the phone," and continued to look around to make sure the coast was clear. She had already left two messages, and received no answers.

Karl had cut off his cell phone so he wouldn't be interrupted. Today could be his last day dealing with Krissy, and he wanted to enjoy himself. The phone rang again, and Karl got angry. Annoyed, he reached over and pulled the cord out of the wall. He rolled over, "Lindy, I'm not talking to anyone else but *you* right now. I would leave Krissy in a heartbeat if I thought we could be together."

Lindy looked uneasy by the disruption and tried to make him think, "Karl she may become concerned if you don't answer." She wondered if he had lost his mind. Surely, he didn't think she would take his non-working self in and take care of him. Ms. Lindy was definitely not that kind of a girl. "Karl, I'm not seeing anyone else. Yes, I like you, but I'm not interested in a relationship with anyone right now. You are a married man with a child. I spend all of my time working, taking care of my mother, and going to school. That is what I look forward to everyday. Now, can I fill your prescription?"

Karl took her response as a *no,* and instructed his Geisha Girl to begin his therapy. Lindy immediately returned to character and obeyed. Karl realized he had fallen in love with this woman, but she didn't want to be with him. He was just an appointment to her, and his time had run out. Thinking about his life, he knew that he was tired and it was time to check out.

After Lindy's departure, Karl stared out the window, and wondered what his next step should be. It sure was a beautiful day, but he was going to bring grief to his family. Sitting on the side of the bed, he knew that Krissy would know he hadn't paid the mortgage in three months, and she would be moving in with her parents. She would question him about what he did with the money. Not wanting to deal with her or her father, he knew he had to do something. Clothing the curtains, he dressed and drove to the neighborhood park.

Sitting in his car he thought, "I can't continue to live like this. I either have to get a job, be a husband and father, or move on. Otherwise, I may as well not be with anyone. I thought Lindy was in love with me. I have been seeing this woman, and financially enrolling her for almost a year. I now realize she has been treating me like a business deal, and I'm in love by myself. I definitely don't love Krissy, but I care about her. I'm just an inconvenience to everybody. She was the one that wanted children, because I sure didn't. I already had a son that I didn't want to be bothered with."

Ironically, crumb snatchers and free loaders were not his style. Without hesitating, he reached underneath his car seat, grabbed his gun, placed the muzzle to his temple (laughed aloud), and pulled the trigger screaming! "Bye Life."

Krissy was packing up for the day when the phone rang, "Hello, yes this is Karl Windsor's wife." After hearing what Karl had done she had screamed, fainted, and collapsed to the floor." Although not sure of what was happening, Priza, and her other team members came running after hearing her screams. Priza picked up the phone and spoke with the police department, and gasped in shock.

The company nurse cradled Krissy's head and applied the smelling salts until she finally opened her eyes. Through sobs, she told them, "Karl is at County General after attempting suicide. Please, can someone call and ask my parents to pick up Hannah? Please, I need a ride to the hospital. He's still alive." Lish grabbed her purse, and escorted Krissy to the parking structure. Blindly walking to Lish's car, Krissy had gotten in and sat quietly as they drove to the hospital.

The office was abuzz with conversation on Karl's suicide attempt and Krissy's fainting. Meanwhile, Krissy and Lish arrived on "2 west," and were met by Karl's attending doctor and nurse. They ushered her toward Karl's room, and the doctor spoke empathetically, "Mrs. Windsor, we are sorry. Right now, he's alive and that's about all we can say. We have stabilized him, by placing him on a respirator. The neurosurgeon exposed portions of his brain to allow expansion." Walking into the room, Krissy inhaled when she saw Karl, because his face was horribly swollen, and unrecognizable. The top of his head was covered in bandages and red tinged. Krissy wavered, and Lish quickly sat her down. Krissy's dad walked in at that moment, looked at Karl, and proceeded to comfort his daughter. He wondered what Karl had done this time.

Meanwhile, Lindy had pulled up to her home and realized that she was unkempt from the session. She quickly tidied herself before entering her house, and hoped Karl had sense enough to tidy up after their session. However, maybe this was what Krissy needed to get on with her life. Out of all of her clients, Karl was the worst. No motivation, no ambition, and definitely not that great in bed. A full session of the missionary style was a lot to handle, but for five hundred dollars, at least she got a chance to relax and plan the rest of her day. The only pleasure she got was when he allowed her to take over.

She always put her best foot forward hoping he would meet her there and increase his capabilities,

"He's physically challenged, but I'm still tight and definitely right. Thank you Kandi for *Bedroom Kandi*, Girl! Those balls work perfectly. Good Luck, Krissy because you will definitely need it. Contract Terminated!"

3 DAWN, "HE'S SHY"

Dawn sat in Alexandria's office, and a beautiful office it was. Alexandria had impeccable taste, and the solid cherry wood desk was beautiful. Her goldfish Harley and Charlie complimented it.

"Alexandria, I need this job and a second job. My husband works hard and tries to support us, but he's unable to find steady employment. You see, he's very shy. Just this morning, he left before I got up, and went down to the blood bank. He goes down there two times per week and brings home a little money. It really helps with the little things. My salary covers our mortgage, and I provide him a household allowance. Together we make it work. My daughter, Belle, is in and out, and now she's expecting. Bence isn't her father, but he treats her like his own daughter. He takes care of her while I'm at work. He makes sure she's eating right, and taking care of herself and the baby."

Dawn quickly shifted gears and asked, "Alexandria, what can I do? I have been volunteering for overtime, but it's still not enough. Bence says the bills are getting higher and he may need close to eight hundred dollars per week to keep us afloat."

Alexandria was preoccupied with her own situation, and wished Dawn had spoken with Priza, "Dawn, I don't really know what to tell you. All of your children are adults now. I know Belle is expecting, but she has always been an independent girl. Maybe it's time to prepare her for motherhood. You also should hold Bence accountable, or let him move on. Without Bence, you could afford to take care of yourself, and alleviate some worry. Let him

go, girl! Not tomorrow, let him go today. Bring Belle

home, because she needs you right now. Besides, you

pay her rent every month. It's time to celebrate

because you will be the first of us to become a

grandmother. By the way, did Bence ever get his

green card?"

Back at Dawn's house, Belle sat in her car and

watched her mother to leave. Hastily, she got out of

her car, and walked into the house. "Hey Bence! I

watched her leave, so I knew it was okay to come in."

Belle walked over and kissed Bence on the lips and he

hungrily returned her kiss. "Bence, we have to tell

mama sometime soon. I'm going to have this baby,

and I will need your help. You have told me many

times you love me, but you keep staying with her.

Why don't you leave so she can find someone else? I

love my mama, but I need you more. By the way, it's a boy and he will be here in three months."

Bence lifted Belle up into his arms and carried her upstairs to her mother's bed. With her head in his chest, and his lips caressing her hair he reached the bed. Bence carefully placed her in the center of the bed, and gave in to her demands.

Sometimes later, Bence placed his hand over his eyes, "Belle, we can't do this anymore. None of this should've happened. We made a mistake and it has turned into much more. We have to tell Dawn the truth and maybe she will forgive us. Maybe Dawn and I can raise the baby and you can move on. You are only nineteen years old, and you have your whole life ahead of you. Besides, I don't know if this is my baby or not."

Belle sat up sharply and began to put on her clothes. "You know this is your baby, we have been sleeping together since you came to my bed two years ago and forced yourself on me. I didn't want you then, but after you came to me for so long, you grew on me. I liked what happened to me when we were together, and I'm not willing to give it up. We have been meeting all this time and you have the nerve to deny my baby. I'm surprised mama hasn't figured it out. Feeling guilty, I moved out when I was eighteen years old, but you came to my apartment to be with me. You even said you would leave her for me."

"Belle please, you forced yourself on me, and I know it doesn't excuse my behavior but you did. I'm fifty-five years old and way too mature for you. I do love you, but not like that. I'm addicted to what you do to me, but I'm married to your mother. I never said I would leave Dawn for you. When I'm with you, my body becomes lustful, but nothing more. I can't deny the chemistry between us, but this has to stop."

Belle slowly walked toward Bence. "You love me, I know you do."

Bence returned to attention and reluctantly played with her again. Overcome with need and longing for attention, he pulled Belle close. "Belle, I don't love you like that. I don't, and this is the last time, I mean it."

Dawn sat in her cubicle visiting with Gabby, when Gabby asked, "I'm new at marriage, but I have to ask, what is wrong with these men? I just don't understand it. My father worked, and my brothers still work, but my husband insist he's disabled."

Gabby stared at Dawn, and asked, "Ms. Dawn, can you answer that question for me?"

Dawn was feeling extremely uncomfortable but answered, "I don't know. I can't help you, because I need help myself. You are too young for your life to be a mess. Go home to your parents." Instantly, Dawn wondered what Bence was doing.

Finally, Belle left. Bence cleaned the house, showered, and was dressing when the doorbell rang. He finished dressing, walked toward the door, and prayed it wasn't Belle returning for round four. Against his better judgment, he'd done exactly what she'd asked of him. He knew it was time to put an end to this Belle business. He felt so defeated about the whole situation, and knew he was a better man than this. Bence felt his boldness return as he opened the door. Standing in front of him was his weekly appointment, in which he had forgotten.

Lindy noticed the rise, and rubbed her knee against his thigh. "Hi Bence, sorry I'm late. I had to take care of my mother, until her caregiver arrived. I see you are at attention. Oh! I saw your stepdaughter leave so I waited until the coast was clear. She's pregnant isn't she?"

Bence stuttered as Lindy touched his forearm, "Hi Lindy, I have to reschedule, because I was up late last night, and I'm tired. Yes, that was my stepdaughter and yes, she's pregnant. Being young and immature, she messed around, and now she's pregnant. Dawn likes me to look after her."

Lindy knew Bence carried on with his stepdaughter, because she had observed them through the window, and on several occasions. She always waited until the stepdaughter left before knocking on the door. "I empathize, but I still need my money it's seven hundred and fifty dollars. If you cancel, you still have to pay me today, but I can reschedule you for next week."

Sighing deeply and tired from his earlier encounter, he removed Lindy's hand from his arm. Bence walked over to the armoire, removed the money from the household expense jar, and counted out her money. "Here take it and I will see you next week."

Lindy looked forward to her time with him, and his love prescription. He had requested his weekly cat-woman, and she obliged. Lindy purred and began her cat woman dance. Inviting him over, she patted the sofa beside her, and purred again. Lindy didn't feel like rescheduling, besides she was looking forward to their session.

Bence having just showered from his early meeting with Belle thought, "Well, I did pay for it, so I may as well enjoy myself." Bence began to remove his clothes and walked to the couch.

Minutes later, he raised his head and remarked, "Very sweet, I love you Dawn," and kissed her lips. Hurriedly and with a new burst of energy, he didn't disappoint.

Realizing that Bence had called her "Dawn" Lindy laughed to herself and thought, "Yes, Dawn has it like that." At least he still loved his wife, outside of the stepdaughter business, which wasn't her concern. She really hoped he landed on his feet, after this "baby mama drama" mess.

Out of all of her clients, she knew Bence was really

a good person, and she knew he loved Dawn.

4 _G_ABRIELLE, "HE'S DISABLED" ◆

It was a beautiful morning, and not a cloud in the sky. Stepping over the water puddles from the sprinklers, Gabby hurried up the sidewalk and glanced toward her office window. She glanced at her watch, realized she was late, and knew it would be cloudy inside the building. They had to know she was doing the best she could and if not, what fricking ever! Walking through the lobby, she acknowledged the receptionist and her being seven minutes late. The phones were ringing and chatter was flowing through the air.

Gabby followed the same routine everyday, and woke up at four thirty in the morning. She performed her wifely duties by playing restaurant host, showering, and dressing for work. She couldn't deny that her husband, Reese, served her very well, but he just wouldn't work. She barely had enough time to get to work after their early morning sex-scapades. She was late twice last week and Priza had counseled her six times already. If she lost her job, they wouldn't have anything. Thinking about why she was late, she smiled, "Well, who wouldn't like the reception she received every morning?"

Priza stared as Gabby ran to her desk and hurriedly logged in. Watching, she quickly summoned her to her office. Gabby was a beautiful young girl, with the cutest freckles and prettiest hair she had ever seen. Unfortunately, she knew she had to do something with this late business, and she felt bad. She had tried to help her, but she wasn't taking her position serious. She had only been with the company a few months, and was doing the same thing every week.

Gabby logged out and walked to Priza's office, "Good morning, Ms. Priza, I'm sorry I'm late again. I am only 22 years old and I don't know many people in this town. I'm self-supporting, and my husband Reese is 23 years old and he's not able to work. He's disabled and I really don't know what to do. We are renting a house from his parent's friends and right now, I'm paying for it by myself. The doctor wrote him a release statement, but he continues to stay at home. We don't have any children, but I think I may be pregnant. You see Ms. Priza, I have to do everything." Taking on a child's role she murmured, "I'm really sorry I'm late."

Priza murmured to herself, "Is this confess to Priza day? I mean, can this many people in one workplace have the same problem?" Staring at

Gabby, she remembered she was the manager,

"Gabby, I don't know you very well, but you are

much too young to be going through so many

changes. But! You were late twice last week, I

counseled you, and told you not to be late again.

Now, you are late again, and you have only been here

six months. Here at LEKO Aeronautics, we provide

first class service for our clients, because they provide

us with jobs. Whether they are purchasing a new

helicopter, or an airplane part, they expect total

quality. Our management team provides total quality

leadership, LEKO demands first class service from all

employees, and you have to be on time to provide it.

With that said I would suggest you go home to your

parents and seek their guidance and assistance."

Gabby quickly looked down. "Look at me Gabby,

remember you just started this job and work as if you want it. If you are late again, I will have to fire you. This is your third warning, the first two were oral, but this is written so please sign it." Priza pushed the paper and pen toward Gabby.

Gabby spoke as she signed the paper, "I don't talk to my parents much, because they're angry right now. They didn't want us to marry, because we were so young."

Priza stood up, insinuating that the meeting was over. Gabby stood up and walked out, "Thank you, Ms. Priza."

Reese was home tidying himself up after having cleaned the house. He was excited about his weekly appointment. He had barely finished when the doorbell rang. He grabbed the phone, "Hi Lindy, I have been thinking about you all morning and I'm so glad you are here. I will be right there."

Although Lindy was older and considered a cougar, she had the body of an eighteen year old. She performed like the Lone Ranger and he was her Tonto. Reese had pawned his wedding band for twelve hundred dollars, so he could pay her five hundred dollars for coming to see him weekly. Last week he'd pawned his car, stolen from Gabby, and lied when she'd questioned him.

Lindy walked in dressed in her Lone Ranger costume and smiled at Reese. "I'm here as your *Lone Rangeress,* but I see you are still putting on your costume." Lindy had on a big white hat, which covered her long black wig, black mask, black body suit, and black knee-high boots.

Reese smoothed his hair to the back and placed the signature small band around his head. He was putting on his brown-fringed vest and pants when Lindy rang the doorbell. He ushered her in and motioned her to the couch, so he could finish preparing, "Excuse me while I continue dressing." Reese hurried back into the bedroom. Standing in the mirror, he knew he had come a long way and was ready to terminate his contract. Lindy had given him a six-month contract, which was dependent on his progress. He always felt guilty because he loved Gabby so much, but until recently, he had been unable to perform as her husband. Therapy had served him well and he was serving Gabby even better.

Lindy sat on the couch and waited for Reese to return. Compared to Mason and Bence, he was her third best. Reese was young and clumsy, but always rose to the occasion. In the beginning, he had been defeated, but now he was ready to move on with his life.

When Reese returned to the living room, Lindy stood up and walked over to him. Slowly she placed her leg in between his legs and cupped his face. She demanded he do the same. "Reese touch my face gently, now kiss my neck, touch my shoulders, yes that's it." Grabbing at his waist, Lindy pulled at his waistband, and Reese buckled at the knees. She loosened his belt and proceeded to expose him. He was so transparent she was sure she could see his prostate gland. Nice, young, strong, and Oh! So wrong. "Reese, you are not ready for me this morning. Remember, this is to help you be a good husband to your wife." Slowly, Lindy prepared him.

After a few minutes, he was ready and anxious to prove it.

Reese was completely juvenile by this time. "Ms. Lindy, I'm ready. We can start."

Lindy smiled, "Reese slow down!" and thought, "Young people are so impatient."

Through a raspy voice, Reese said, "Please I'm ready! I think about you all the time. One session a week is not enough, but it's all I can pay for. It's really helping my marriage."

Lindy quickly and comically returned to reality, and stood up. "Reese, I know you are ready for me, but I need you to pay me before we continue. I can't function for free, so as soon as we complete our transaction, I will take care of you." Gesturing, Lindy explained, "Nothing personal, I love our time together, but I have obligations." Lindy thought to herself, "I provide a service and I'm financially compensated for it. Reese better have my money or I'm out of here!" She always had clients who wanted to milk the cow free, and charity wasn't part of her practice.

Irritated by the interruption, Reese got up and walked over to his wallet, removed five one hundred dollar bills, and placed them in Lindy's hand. Lindy quickly took the money, put it in her purse, and just as quickly, returned to character. After several minutes of instructing him on foreplay, and watching him demonstrate, she realized this would be their last session. After two additional hours of therapy, Lindy departed the residence.

Seated at her desk, Gabby wondered what Reese was doing right now. She loved him so much, and they had made so many plans until that stupid motorcycle accident. Her thoughts were interrupted by the five o'clock bell. Relieved, Gabby stood up and began packing for the day. Walking toward the door, she overheard Priza talking to Elissa, "We are all having the same issues in our home, but we still have a job to do." Gabby liked Elissa because she was so classy, and stayed to herself. Occasionally they had coffee, but they only discussed work. Elissa was very private, and kept her home life to herself.

Meanwhile, Lindy had left Reese sound asleep and snoring. Hurriedly, she departed the home and drove up the street. She had decided to contact the doctor that had referred Reese, because his therapy was complete. Reese was a college graduate, and was fully able to work, and support his home. He was using her as a safety net. Lindy wondered, "What is wrong with this kid? What is he afraid of? I know

he's having good relations with his wife, because he

tells me. He doesn't need me anymore. I'm

terminating this contract to save his life."

Lindy felt sorry for Gabby, because she was too

young to put up with this mess. Driving up the street,

she cut on the radio and sang along with TLC's

Scrubs. She really loved this song, because it put

many of her client's lives into perspective. "What's

wrong with these young people?"

Pulling into the garage, Gabby got out and

walked into the house, "Hi Baby, I missed you

today." Remembering what Lindy taught him. Reese

walked up and kissed her softly, but hungrily. Slowly

he pushed her toward the bedroom and closed the

door behind them. You see, Reese had decided he

was done with Lindy. Besides, he had to get a job so

he could get his car back. Furthermore, it was way too much fricking money to give to a whore.

Six months after the accident, the medication had healed Reese's wounds, but it prevented him from performing his husbandly duties. He had tried his best to stay engaged, but Mr. Happy had been more sad than happy. After finding nothing medically wrong, his doctor recommended Ms. Lindy under the strictest of confidence. Until Ms. Lindy, he had given up, and now he was feeling like himself again.

Still lying in the bed, Reese stared at the sleeping Gabby. She was the only person who still believed in him, and continued to support him. He knew she deserved more than what she was getting. They'd made so many plans when they graduated from college, but everything was on hold. Realizing he was better, Reese had called the hospital to see if his position was still available. That was two days ago, and he was still awaiting a callback. Reaching over he exposed the sleeping Gabby's girls. He nibbled on her until she was fully awake. Looking into her eyes, he realized how much he loved her. He enjoyed his wife and knew she enjoyed him. Although Ms. Lindy was older and a professional, he had enjoyed the training, but was glad he was himself again. Reese had officially graduated. Contract Terminated!

5 ALEXANDRIA, "MAX IS AN ARTIST" ◉

Alexandria was ecstatic and as marketing manager, her department was dominating the company's other departments, even Priza's. According to Priza, her employees were too busy with marital problems and not working as hard as she would have liked.

Priza sat in Alexandria's office across from her as Alexandria smugly announced her latest accomplishment, "Priza, I secured a 21 million dollar contract for the small aircraft department." They high fived and danced together. Through many years, Priza and Alexandria had remained BFF's, excelled at work together, and loved each other like sisters.

Finally, they were through celebrating, and began to discuss stuff on the home front.

"Priza, Max is the father of my children and I love him. Remember the *Starving Artist*. He's an artist and right now, he's down on the boardwalk trying to sell his paintings. He goes down there every day hoping to be discovered. Until then, it's my job to support our family, and take care of the household. I just bought him a new BMW, so he can look the part when he's out there. I can afford it, I make six figures, and my money is his money, right?" Not receiving affirmation from Priza, she continued to talk, "Besides, he looks really good in the new car I bought him. Did Eirik enroll in any classes this semester?" Childishly, Alexandria smiled, and Priza shook her head, and held up her hands in defeat.

While walking out of Alexandria's office, Priza

shouted over her shoulder! "No Eirik hasn't started school yet. It's time we stop justifying their unemployment status, and hold them accountable, I love you Alex." Priza called her "Alex" when they were alone.

Priza thought back to the day Alexandria had met Max on the boardwalk. Although Alexandria came from a tight knit, two-parent home, there was little else for the children, except love and an education. She had defied the odds, went to college, and graduated with honors. Her family was very proud on her. After college, she forewent modeling and secured a management position with one of the best aeronautical companies in the country, along with her college BFF, Priza. Now Mrs. Priza Oliveira.

While in school, she didn't have time for dating because she had to study, but now it was her turn to live. While strolling down the boardwalk, she stopped to admire the paintings of one of the local artist, and the artist himself. She and Priza had seen him right away and immediately set their sights on him. Unknowingly, they had zeroed in on a zero. Alexandria whispered out the side of her mouth, "Certainly, eye candy." He was golden brown, had his wavy hair cropped close, and had the body of a Greek God. No fricking kidding, he was fine! She formally met Mr. Max and her future husband on the boardwalk, that very day.

He caught their stares and walked out in their path. Looking directly at Alexandria, "You are amazingly beautiful, and no disrespect is intended. By the way, I'm Maximillian Stottler, but call me Max. Can I paint your portrait?" He acknowledged Priza and waited for Alexandria's answer.

Standing beside Priza, she had made eye contact and smiled. Nodding yes, she took a seat, as she was flattered. She sat for over an hour while he drew her naturally curly and kinky hair, and Priza browsed the paintings of all the authors.

Alex wore her hair natural, and loved the texture of it. Growing up in the Midwest, all of the girls had worn relaxers, weaves, cornrows, and braids while she had embraced her full head of natural hair. Her mother, a native Jamaican, had forbidden the chemicals that altered the natural pattern of her hair. According to her mother, "the chemicals in those products change the pattern in your hair, and they change the chemicals in your brain." Alexandria had been satisfied with her mother's rationale and never questioned it. The painting was a great likeness of her, and she tried to pay him for his time. Max refused, insisted that she take it as a gift in exchange

for a future date, and Alexandria agreed.

After that first meeting, she had gone to the

boardwalk daily for a week. On one particular

Saturday, she was down at the boardwalk to have

lunch with her friends. Passing by his kiosk, she had

waved and kept going. Max was busy painting a

young light-haired girl, had waved back, and

continued painting. Uncomfortable with the sight at

Max's station, she had snared her nose, and continued

toward the restaurant.

Nearing the restaurant's steps, she felt a tap on

her shoulder. Turning around, she'd almost bumped

into Max, who was standing close upon her. She

looked toward his station and found it deserted. He

had abandoned his station and hurried behind her.

Holding Alexandria's hand, he asked, "Can I take you

to lunch or join you and your friends?"

Alexandria abandoned her friends. During lunch, she learned that Max came from Boston and had come west to attend college. He had completed two years of college, and dropped out to pursue his painting career. After several years, Max was still on the boardwalk, and continued to peddle his paintings. Confident of his skills and appearance, he felt a breakthrough was inevitable. Born from mixed heritage, Max was mulatto, which explained his golden brown skin and wavy cropped hair.

During lunch, he'd officially invited her on a second date, and she'd happily accepted. Their second date happened one week later, but not on the boardwalk. Anticipating his arrival, Alexandria sat by the window of her studio apartment, and looked through the curtains. She lived ten minutes from the boardwalk, but wasn't sure where he lived. Max arrived in his yellow convertible Volkswagen, Alexandria quickly closed the curtain, and waited for his knock.

On their second date, he took her to a wonderful Ethiopian restaurant in the city, and she immediately fell in love with the food and the atmosphere. It was a completely new world for her.

On their third date, they hung out at the boardwalk while he worked. She introduced him to Jamaican food, by delivering it to his kiosk. While waiting, she encountered a male coworker, and hugged and kissed him on the check.

Later, Max became enraged, called her a whore, and slapped her across the face. Alexandria placed her hand to her face, because she was without words.

Shocked, she vowed to never speak to him again. He had pleaded and apologized for over two weeks before she agreed to see him again. Max continued to give her an occasional slap when he wasn't happy with her. She purposely neglected to tell Priza about the abuse, fearing her response, besides Max was just jealous. After a year of being slap free, they tied the knot back in her hometown. The first few years were great, followed by Maxie's arrival, and later Ms. Sari.

Knowing that Alexandria and Max shared a family with responsibilities, Priza was shocked that Alexandria didn't hold Max accountable. Priza sat at her desk and recalled another of their conversations in Alexandria's office. "Alexandria, you've been married fourteen years and for most of those years, you have been the sole provider for your family. You have never once told me he provided a steady income. I regret the day you met him. We should've kept walking. It's not up to me to decide if it's right or wrong. Maybe you should rethink things, your children are in school, and you take care of everybody anyway. Maybe he should get a regular job and paint as a hobby. Look at you! You are sporting Louis Vuitton luggage beneath your eyes. You have been working sixty hours every single week for as long as I can remember. You need to make some changes. So my question to you is, *is it right, or is it wrong?*"

Infuriated by the truth, Alexandria only saw red and began to cry blood tears. She knew Max wasn't the man he should've been, but he was her husband and her children's father.

Alexandria spoke with her mother weekly and carefully skirted around Max's employment status. If her family knew everything, they wouldn't be happy with her living situation.

Priza had left Alexandria's office very disturbed, and worried about her friend. Alex was the best friend in the world, and had a heart of gold. She was held in the highest regard amongst her peers, but her private life mimicked hell. Out of all of the management staff, Alexandria had the best office in the building, with her own private entrance. Although she hadn't seen anymore bruises, Priza wondered if Alex was still being abused.

Priza had noticed Alex's bruises years ago, and had asked her if Max was abusive. Alex denied it, so Priza chose to forget it, and now she was sorry.

Lindy was speaking with Max on the phone to obtain his love prescription. "Good morning, Max. What's your love prescription for today?" Lindy sighed because Max always wanted to paint strawberries and chocolates on her. He would consume her until all of the red and brown was gone. Today, she was hoping for a different prescription.

"Lindy, you know what I like. I want you in the red lingerie and red pumps, and please wear the strawberry blonde wig. I will cover you with chocolate, spread on some strawberries, and then I will paint your picture." Max was getting excited just thinking about it. This woman was his dream come true, and he requested the same fantasy every week. It was getting harder to keep up with the payments, but he would find a way. People on the boardwalk weren't stopping as often to have their pictures painted, nor were they buying as much. He knew he should expand his work, or business would continue to fall, and Alexandria would stay on his back.

Lindy took extra care to fulfill Max's prescription, because he could be mean if she missed a beat. She carefully dressed in the red lingerie with red shoes that he always requested. She carried her strawberry blonde wig with her, and put it on in the car, to avoid unnecessary questions. Max enjoyed how her strawberry tresses fell to her waist. Lindy grabbed her purse, trench coat, and incidentals and left her home. She still took great care to avoid her mother and her caregivers when she dressed for her clients. She didn't like having to explain why she was made up to look like someone else. Sometimes her mother would interrupt her and fire off with a million questions. Sitting in the driver's seat, she donned her wig. She pointedly looked into the rear view mirror and didn't recognize herself.

Finally arriving at Max's house, Lindy parked in

the back and walked upto the back door. Max opened the door and salivated at the sight of her. He invited her in, and she crossed into Alexandria's home. She sat on the sofa and Max sat next to her and began to make excuses for not having last week's and this week's payment.

Lindy interrupted him, "Max, unless you pay me one thousand dollars today, I will have to delete you from my roster. I'm a businesswoman, you signed a one-year contract, and I expect you to uphold your part of the agreement. It's only one more month and your contract will be over." Thank goodness, thought Lindy.

Grabbing Lindy's hand, Max spoke, "I would have to give you part of our mortgage money, and Alexandria will be angry with me if I don't pay it. My weekly allowance is just enough, and I hustle for the remainder of your fee. I can give you five hundred today and five hundred next week."

Lindy stood up and smiled sweetly, "I will see you in court. Shall I send the summons here or to Alexandria's workplace? After all, I'm providing the both of you a service." Lindy sighed because she hated going through this with Max every single week. She had decided she would terminate his contract today after receiving her money. Thank goodness! She had enacted that one clause for all clients. She could terminate any contract at will, and release her clients from their obligations. She wouldn't miss the discomfort that went along with Max, since he was extremely endowed, which wasn't to her taste! Smiling she thought, "Good luck, Alexandria, you are going to need it."

Max stood up glaring at her, "Okay! I don't

understand you, I have paid you faithfully for over ten months, and every time I come up short, you threaten me. We both enjoy what we do here. Anyway, here's your money, now show me some kindness."

Reaching over to grab her money, Lindy counted all of it. Assured of the correct amount, she changed her demeanor. "Max you have always been my favorite, where would you like to start?" Lindy dropped her coat and stood in the front of Max. "Did I fulfill your love prescription?"

Max nodded and bit through the red lingerie. Alexandria flinched, "Ouch! Take it easy with my girls, and treat them with respect."

Max lessened his hold. "Much better, I like that." Shoving her to the floor, he sat at the easel and painted her portrait. Directly after the painting, Max received his therapy. She had appeased him frontwards, backwards, and badgered him some more. After all, the girl had to go out with a bang and finally, he arrived. "That was great, Max! I mean really great!" Lying quietly, he didn't speak for several minutes until Lindy crawled across the floor reaching for her clothes.

Max grabbed her leg, "Wait! I have another fifteen minutes with you and I want my monies worth." Lindy looked underneath her legs and Max was at the green light. She sighed deeply noticing his metal mushroom. Lindy braced herself and completed their session. Weakened, they both fell asleep on the floor, because they'd never made it past the living room.

LEKO Aeronautics was in full motion as Alexandria gathered her belonging and prepared to go home. "Priza, I think I'll go home and surprise my husband, before the kids get home from school. I will see you tomorrow."

Max and Lindy were asleep on the living room floor, when Max woke up to the sound of the key in the door. Frantically, Max shook Lindy awake whispering, "Get your stuff, and get out of here, Alex is coming through the front door." Lindy grabbed her clothes, and ran to the back of the house. She quickly donned her clothes, opened the door, and slipped out. Oops! She had forgotten her underwear, and hoped Max had enough sense to hide them. She slinked down the side of the house, jumped in Naomi, and bid them both farewell (her panties and Max). CONTRACT TERMINATED!

Alexandria stopped at the mall to allow the children time to get home, after deciding she didn't want to entertain Max alone. An hour later, she

unlocked the door and walked inside the foyer.

"Max, Sari, Maxie, I'm home!" Throwing her keys on

the hallway table and tired from a long day,

Alexandria sighed, "Oh Boy!" While standing at the

base of the stairwell, Sari appeared, ran down, and

jumped from the third stair right into her arms, nearly

knocking her breathless. This kid was only four years

old and had the energy of a marathon runner.

Alexandria loved Sari and Maxie more than anything

in this world, including Max.

"Mommy! Mommy!" Sari laughed as she placed

sloppy wet kisses all over Alexandria's face.

Hearing the noise, twelve-year-old Maxie came

downstairs, and hugged her, "Hi Mom, what's for

dinner?" Alexandria looked at Maxie, noticed he was

taller than Max, and how much she loved him. He

had the same good looks as Max, but was even more handsome.

Alexandria believed her children were the picture of perfection and filled with innocence. "Gee, Thanks! Can I get in the house first and where's your dad?" Awkward silence followed.

Sari was still wrapped around Alexandria's waist, and had a tight hold on her hair. "Daddy was butt naked Mommy. He was bathtub ready and lying on the floor when we got home." Alexandria smiled as Sari had used her "bathtub ready" on her dad.

Max shifted nervously because he had seen his dad sleeping on the floor with the woman, and had quietly stepped back outside. Maxie ran next door to the neighbor, retrieved Sari from the neighbor, and went back to their front door. He had noisily inserted the key into the door lock to awaken them. Seeing the pain in Maxie's eyes, Alexandria took control of the situation.

Alexandria kissed her daughter, "Sari go back upstairs and play in your room until dinner. I will come get you when it's ready." Sari jumped down and ran up to her room. Maxie started up the stairs behind her, but Alexandria quickly grabbed his arm.

"Wait Maxie." Alexandria waited until Sari was out of earshot. "Was your dad naked?" Alexandria looked into his eyes, "It's okay, you can tell me the truth."

Tearing up, Maxie started to speak, "When I got home from school, dad was lying on the floor with this woman they both were naked and sleeping. So, I stepped back out, and went next door to get Sari.

When I got back, I rattled the keys so dad would know I was home. When we stepped inside, Dad was naked with a sheet around him, but the woman ran to the back door and left." Maxie began to cry. "I didn't know Sari saw them, I tried to protect her. I'm sorry Mom, I hate him, and it's not the first time I've seen them. She comes here every Wednesday and they have sex." Maxie was fully crying and shaking at this time. Numb from what she had just heard, Alexandria grabbed her son and kissed the top of his head. Alexandria turned him toward her, "Maxie it's okay, I promise you it will be okay. I'm going to make everything alright." Still hugging him, she continued to kiss the top of his head while she cried. Unbeknown to the both of them, Max was standing at the top of the stairs listening from the shadows. Alexandria pushed Maxie away, "Go upstairs and take

Sari to the TV room, and don't come down until I call you."

Alexandria sat on the couch and cried softly until she felt a hand on top of her head. She looked up and Max was stroking her hair. "Alexandria, what's wrong? Why are you crying?"

Alexandria spoke angrily, "Stop it! Don't touch me. How long has all of this been going on? Is this why you need so much money to run our household? Need to take care of your woman friend, and keep her happy. With my money! Is that it? I have been taking care of you for fourteen years. Thank you for appreciating me by disrespecting me."

Max tried to interrupt, "Maxie is wrong, it's not what you think. She's nothing to me. It was only sex."

Alexandria had considered divorcing Max several times and this had sealed the deal. "Stop it! Don't you dare try to discredit our child. You will not undermine him, because I won't allow it. YOU'RE DONE! WE'RE DONE! Get the hell out of my house. I've taken care of you, supported you, loved you, and you have brought shame into my home. Yes, my home, the one I bought and pay for without your help. I want you out of here tonight."

Max was unsure of how to respond, because he had nowhere to go. Before marrying Alexandria, he had lived as a hobo with the other artist. He had spent many nights at her apartment, but she'd never stayed at his place. When asked where he lived, he would always change the subject.

Looking for someone to blame he thought about Lindy and how she had ruined his life.

Although beautiful, Lindy was just a high price whore, and he didn't even like her. He should've quit when he was ahead. Unsure how to proceed, he decided he would go commando, "Look, I have put up with you telling me what to do for years and I'm not going anywhere. I'm staying here with you and our children." He slapped Alexandria across the face, straddled, and tried to choke her.

Hearing the screams from upstairs, Maxie and Sari ran toward their mother's screams. Arriving downstairs, Maxie jumped on Max's back, while Sari commenced to biting him. While crying, Sari screamed, "Leave my mommy alone!"

Max released Alexandria and stood up. He roughly flung Maxie against the wall, and shook Sari off his leg. Then he stopped, realizing he was assaulting his wife and children. Grabbing his head,

Max turned to each of them and cried, "I'm so sorry."
Max realized he'd become the person he was years
ago, when he would abuse Alex and apologize later.
After they'd married, he promised he'd never hit her
again and until now, he hadn't.

Alexandria coughed and held her throat, "Get
the hell out of here or I will call the police." In
shock, Max walked out of their lives.

Alexandria leaned back and felt a lump under her
head. Turning she realized it was a pair of panties.
She'd found Lindy's underwear. Cringing, Alexandria
flung them and shouted, "Home wrecking trash!"
Alexandria gathered her children, and they cried.

6 BA'MYNN, "I'M NOT GOING ANYWHERE" •

Ba'Mynn's father, who hailed from the Republic of Ghana, had been very strict on her and her siblings. After Ba'Mynn became pregnant, he had refused to speak to her, and immediately removed her from his home. Ba'Mynn's mother reluctantly agreed to evict her, and she was out on her own. She blamed herself for allowing Ba'Mynn to go to that dance. You see, BaMynn's parents couldn't afford the embarrassment of an unwed daughter, or the negative influence over their younger children. Ba'Mynn should've known better because she was reared in a home of respect and love. Telling it like it T I S and putting it soundly, "Ba'Mynn had to go."

Left without anywhere to go, Ba'Mynn had moved in with one of her teachers, Mrs. Ross. Six months later, Ba'Mynn gave birth to her baby boy, Brent. Two months later, she graduated from an alternative high school at the top of her class. Mrs. Ross and her family sat in the audience and cheered her on. Ba'Mynn had blown kisses as she received her diploma. They were truly her family and she loved them.

At Mrs. Ross's insistence, Ba'Mynn had stayed another year. During that year, she went to a technical school, and became a computer technician. A week after her graduation, she'd secured a decent job, and moved out with one-year-old Brent. She would be forever grateful to Mrs. Ross, as she had been so kind and supportive. Mrs. Ross had been what a mother should've been when their child was in trouble. She spent holidays with them, because they were her family. Her real parents were nonexistent.

Ba'Mynn had never reconnected with her parents, but her biological siblings had reclaimed their relationship with her after they graduated from high school. Now Mason, Brent's father, was another story.

When Mason found out she was pregnant, he had promised he would take care of her, but had disappeared. If only she had said "no" to Mason, she still would have had her parents in her life. Mason had lied and said everything would be okay but failed her miserably. After moving out on her own, he reappeared unexpectedly. Sadly, she had allowed him to move in with her. He agreed to pay his share of the bills, and help with Brent. Although sporadic, having the extra help with additional income and babysitting had improved her living situation. Still working, Ba'Mynn returned to school, and finished her college degree. The day after her graduation, and against her better judgment she had married Mason. Before their marriage, he had worked in construction, but quit a month after moving in with her. He continued to stay home with baby Brent, while Ba'Mynn slayed the dragons. Years later, he was still staying home, and working and hustling when he wanted to. It was a struggle watching him stay home in the mornings, but he cared for the kids. Yes kids! Ba'Mynn had delivered a set of twins and they were now six years old, Myles and Mya.

Work was slow at LEKO Aeronautics, so Ba'Mynn went to visit Priza, "Girl this has been going on for years, and he still won't work. Frankly, I don't know what to do anymore. He's a grown man with a family. If I had listened to Mrs. Ross, I wouldn't be in this mess. And get this, he thinks struggling and hustling is a career," sighed Ba'Mynn. "Mason came from a broken home and his father wasn't there for him and his younger brother. His mother raised them on her own, and she was always working up until she got sick. Mason was fourteen and Darrick was ten years old when she passed away. Immediately, they were shipped off to foster care, and stayed until they were of legal age.

In the midst of all of this, and at fifteen years of age, Mason was caught stealing and was taken to juvenile hall. His current foster family refused to take him back, and he was shipped to a different foster home, alone. Darrick was left to fend for himself, and they had lost contact.

Mason barely missed being caught up in the correctional system. After juvenile hall, he was scared straight and behaved until he finished high school. "I met him at a high school dance. He was there with another girl, but spent the evening coddling me. I was so naïve, and he preyed on it. Story of my life, that's how Brent got here. I thought he would want better for his children, but none of this seems to matter to him. I mean he lived with strangers and practically raised himself."

Priza stared at Ba'Mynn before replying, "Why do you keep putting up with it? None of this makes any sense. You have some hard decisions that only you can make and I would make them soon. You have a son in college and two six year olds at home. You have to make the right decision for all of you. Sometimes you have to leave a person to allow them to find themselves, and once they find themselves, they can find you. If it's meant to be things will work out."

Followed by an uncomfortable silence, and disregarding Priza's last comment, Ba'Mynn finally spoke, "I know, you are right. I asked him to register with the local employment agency to pick up some extra money. He got so angry I thought he was going to hit me, but he backed off. Everything I earn goes toward our bills, and keeping us afloat. While he hangs out with his friends everyday. Two years ago, he was on a construction job for five months. I was starting to feel secure, so we bought a new house, and he quit working one month after we moved in. Mason has never held a job longer than six months. Sometimes when things get bad, he scrapes up money to keep us afloat. He sells aluminum can, scrap metal, instruments, blood, and anything else he can get his hands on. You name it he sells it, but he doesn't break the law. I ask Mrs. Ross to speak with him and he told her he was above working for an employment agency. Mason felt I should be glad I had a man at home with me. A couple of years ago, when we got our income tax refund, he purchased a second-hand boat. Excuse me! My income tax refund, because he didn't work that year. He sails once a week for 24 hours and returns home exhausted. I have been on board a few times, but he's never taken me out on it. He uses my money to keep it going."

Bothered by what she had just heard, Priza looked at Ba'Mynn, she was such a sweet young woman, but she wore her heart on her sleeve. "Ba'Mynn, I really think you should reassess your life and decide what's best for you and the children.

There isn't a lot I can tell you, but maybe talk to your family or a therapist. I know you have siblings; maybe they can support you in making the best decision. As your manager, there is nothing I can say or do to make you feel better. Please call the EAS and get some assistance." Priza gave Ba'Mynn an EAS card.

Twiddling her thumbs, Ba'Mynn breathed, "I know Ms. Priza, but I thank you for listening to me. Sometimes, I just have to talk to someone to keep from going crazy. A couple of years ago, we didn't even have food, and I had to look in my children's eyes and watch them cry. When I was laid off from my other job, I went out and stole some food for my babies. I regretted my actions, so when I got my first paycheck I took money to the store manager. I pretended I had found it inside the store. I felt better after I'd replaced what I'd taken."

Ba'Mynn continued her venting, "Mason is going out on his boat this evening, so it will be me and the kids. We have been through so much, and I still have to ask him, when are you getting a job? Ms. Priza, your husband works, everybody else's husband work, but why won't my husband work?"

Ba'Mynn stood up, "I'll see you tomorrow, and have a good evening. I'm sick and tired of being sick and tired. Ms. Priza, I can't leave him, he's my husband, and my children's father." Ba'Mynn walked away but didn't notice the tears in Priza eyes. Ba'Mynn was one of her best employees and it hurt to know she was carrying so much pain. Priza had heard that "tired" phrase before from another employee.

Mason was home packing his overnight bag, and

his gin and juice for his weekly boat trip with Ms. Lindy. He was going to get unfastened tonight. He had sold some stuff out of storage, had money for his family, a little bit to save, and four weekly visits of pleasure with Ms. Lindy.

"Mason how was your day?" Mason, Ba'Mynn, and the twins were sitting at the dinner table finishing supper. Ba'Mynn noticed how cheerful and happy he was, and felt her anger rising. Looking at the children she thought how blessed she was supposed to be, to have her children's father in their home. "Myles, Mya put your plates away, go upstairs, and get ready for your baths." Having twin six-year-olds was a full time job, and she received little assistance from Mason although he was home all day. Most days, they stayed in the afterschool program until Ba'Mynn got off work, while Mason sat home all day. Looking straight at her husband, she cautiously spoke to him, "Mason, I tried calling you today and I couldn't reach you." Facetiously optimistic she asked, "Were you out job-hunting today? You know Brent is in college, Myles is beginning to understand, and you should be setting an example for them instead of sitting at home. Furthermore, I don't want to hear about you not wanting to work for the man anymore. I work for THE MAN all day long, every day." She sarcastically asked, "Will you need gas money for your boat this evening?" Ba'Mynn teared up and stared at him. When asked to find a job, Mason always played on her sympathy about his workplace abuse, and nobody understood him.

He'd totally expected this, so he had his lie ready. "As a matter of fact, I did hustle up some money today. I rented my motorcycle out for three months,

113

so I have gas money and money to put toward the household. Here is six thousand dollars and yes there will be more." Mason placed the money envelope on the table in front of Ba'Mynn, "Send Brent something at college, tell him it's from his dad and I love him."

Feeling guilty for suspecting something shady, she jumped up and kissed him. "Oh baby, thank you. I love you so much because you always come through for us. Will you still be going out on the boat tonight or can I give you something to show my appreciation?" Ba'Mynn walked up, and kissed him on the lips.

Knowing a sexual encounter would make him late getting to the boat and to Lindy, he tried to turn her off. "Oh baby, I'm a little tired from the day and I always go out on the boat, it's my man time. The kids are waiting for us to run their bath water."

Ignoring him, Ba'Mynn kept caressing until she felt some progress. Stepping backwards, Ba'Mynn disrobed and invited him over. "The kids can wait. Besides, they know to sit in their rooms until we come up. Come here, Mason. I have something for you." Ba'Mynn had that look in her eyes.

Mumbling to himself about being late, Mason indulged on her. She was still very sweet. Groaning about being late, he knew he had to do something or he would be stuck. Playing nice, he appeased his wife. He couldn't deny the chemistry between them. Moreover, after their many years together, he still cared about her. He was her first and only, and he did care for her and their children, but he wasn't in love with her. Besides, he had to make his appointment within the next thirty minutes.

Finally, she arrived and he followed shortly

thereafter. Jumping up, he straightened his clothes, and grabbed his bag, "I have to get to the boat. I don't want to miss the high tides. Can you handle the kids from here? I will call you when I get to the boat."

Smiling, Ba'Mynn nodded at him. "Yes, I have the kids and I will see you tomorrow evening. I will wait for your call, now go, and do whatever it's you do on that freaking boat." Ba'Mynn put her clothes back on, climbed up, and sat at the table. She sat and watched her husband grab his overnight bag and rush out of the house for his weekly outing. To this day, she still didn't know what he did on it. It was parked at the local boat arena on row 15E. Suddenly she had an idea, she would bathe the kids, take them next door, she would go down to the boat, and pick up where they left off. She felt her insides swell and she wanted to finish what they had started. Meanwhile, Mason was nearing his exit ramp.

Mason pulled into the boat arena parking lot, grabbed his bag, and ran down the ramp to his boat. As he entered the boat, he realized he still had fifteen minutes to spare before Lindy arrived. Lindy brought out things in him that Ba'Mynn wouldn't understand. When he was with her, he felt like a man. Just saying her name made him stretch. He really cared about Ba'Mynn, but only as his children's mother, and loved her as a friend. They had just been kids when they hooked up.

Mason focused his attention back to Lindy. He had to admit that this woman did things to him that couldn't be of this world. Walking into the bedroom, he started to peel away his clothes so he could take a shower and freshen up. As he turned toward the bed, he noticed a lump in his bed. He walked over, stood by the bed, and Lindy uncovered herself. Jumping slightly, he asked, "When did you get here?"

"Boo! It is I. I came a little early so I could prepare for you. I'm so looking forward to our cruise tonight. I brought food and champagne. Come here and give me a kiss." Mason leaned over to kiss her and she pushed him away. "So you indulged in some *wifey* activities before you got here. I want you too, but you need to brush your teeth and take a shower. I want you fresh. I can pull the anchor while you are showering. We have all night and most of tomorrow."

Mason was her most passionate client, and she could take him on for the full trip. Not only that, she enjoyed every bit of it. He could have been her soul mate, and had almost everything she was looking for in a man. She loved everything about his body. They had the most amazing conversations. If ever there was a man for her, Mason was the one.

Unfortunately, he was unavailable because he already had a wife and he definitely needed a job. In fact, he had informed her that when his contract ended, he was going to find a job, and stay home to be the best husband and father he could be. I listened and told him that it was great he was being noble, but please, "Get a real job and help your wife handle the household responsibilities." He had kissed her and smiled, "I have every intention of doing just that."

Mason kissed her forehead, threw her the keys, and headed into the shower. "Oh wait! I have to call Ba'Mynn and let her know I made it safely. I will be out shortly and I will be ready for you." Lindy walked up the ladder, started the boat, and drove out past the first buoy. The boat could not be seen from shore and that was how they liked it.

Mason finally came out of the shower and approached Lindy, who was sitting on the side of the bed. Clad only in a towel, his pecks drove her crazy.

She stood and swayed her hips to Beyoncé's, "Drunk in Love." She gave him a glass of Dom and they took sips. Stepping back, Lindy took the rest of her Dom and threw it all over Mason's body. Mason followed her lead, and reciprocated. Embracing, they started their therapy.

At home, Ba'Mynn had changed her mind about going to the boat arena. She bathed the kids, and they both had fallen asleep while she dressed them. She put them both to bed and headed to her bedroom to shower. So much for chasing romance.

Tomorrow, she would call off from work and serve her husband dinner when he arrived home. Ba'Mynn climbed into bed and shut out the lights, Thursday nights were always quiet and lonely with Mason gone.

Back on the boat, Mason and Lindy woke up after a two-hour nap. They walked upon deck to eat, and drank the rest of the first bottle of Dom. "Lindy you are an incredible woman, why haven't you ever gotten married? I mean, you are the most amazing woman I have ever met. I don't think there is anybody else like you. Another thing, I have been thinking about us, and I want to renew my contract. I don't think I can live without our weekly meetings. I don't even want to think about living without our weekly meetings. I've been on my own for so long, starting from childhood, but it's different now. I feel like I have someone just for me, YOU! What do you think?" Mason waited her response.

Lindy held his hand, "Mason, I have to leave that decision up to you. You just told me you were getting a job and going to do the married thing, and I respect that. However, I have to say you are the most pleasurable man I've ever been with. I will continue as long as you want. You make me feel alive and I don't experience that too often." As she spoke, Mason was eyeing her seductively. Standing up he pushed all of the food to the deck, grabbed Lindy, and began another therapy session. Afterwards, they slept the entire night on the deck next to the dining table.

It was six o'clock Friday morning, when Lindy was awakened by sunlight. She leaned over and shook Mason awake. She could hear his phone ringing downstairs, "Mason your phone is ringing, and you probably should take it." Lindy was genuinely happy when she was with Mason, because she didn't have to pretend to be someone else.

Mason stood up and walked down the ladder to the bedroom. She could hear him talking, but tuned out the conversation. Wanting to shower she waited until he hung up. Confirming that the coast was clear, she walked down the ladder, and watched as Mason sat down on the side of the bed, and pulled her over as she walked by. He hugged her tightly right before they initiated session number three.

An hour later, Mason and Ba'Mynn was showering together, when he felt he should talk to her about his contract, again. "I love you Lindy, you have awaken feelings inside of me that I have never felt. I wanted to end our contract this evening, but I can't. I love my children and I care about Ba'Mynn, but she deserves some happiness. I'm just not the one to give it to her. Lindy, I want that same happiness." Mason almost pleading continued, Ba'Mynn, and I were just kids when we got together. She got pregnant the first night I met her, and I disappeared for a while. Eventually, I stood by her for Brent's sake, but I was never the husband or father I should've been. I'm not the husband she deserves, because she's not the one for me. Now, I know you have to be with the right person, and be in love before you can truly be happy and make someone else happy."

Mason exhaled and continued, "I came from a broken home, and I lost my mother at an early age. My brother joined the military at seventeen years of age and we lost contact. As you can see, I didn't have anybody but Ba'Mynn. I stayed with her for all of the wrong reasons." Mason looked into her eyes and

Lindy saw the pain behind his words. "I love you Lindy, and for the first time in my life, I know what true love is. I have loved nobody outside of my kids, and I love them very much."

Lindy paused before she broke the silence, "Mason, I love you too. You are the most amazing man, I have ever encountered, but you have two small children who needs both of their parents in their lives. I have to admit your unemployment would be an issue for me." Mason reached over to kiss her, but stopped short of her lips.

Suddenly, the boat shook and he pulled away. Mason opened the shower door and reached for his pants. "What was that? Someone is on board, listen, I hear footsteps." Stepping out of the shower and grabbing their clothes, they hastily began to dress. Unfortunately, it was too late! Ba'Mynn climbed down the ladder, and stared at the both of them.

In shock, Mason mumbled, "Ba'Mynn, this is not what you think." Immediately she turned and climbed back up the ladder. Partially dressed, Mason ran up the ladder desperately trying to reach her. He arrived on deck just in time to see her climbing back into the rental boat. Pulling his pants up, he zipped himself and flinched. As the rental boat drove away, Mason looked directly into Ba'Mynn's eyes and took on all her pain. He had never been so sorry in his life, and had never meant to hurt her, but maybe it was for the best.

Lindy stayed downstairs and waited for Mason to return, this wasn't good. They were only weekly lovers, but being caught by the wife wasn't part of the program. She would keep quiet and wait for his cue. Lindy had to say, "Ba'Mynn was a beautiful woman."

Hearing his footsteps, she waited.

Mason came down the ladder and sat on the side of the bed. "Lindy, this has been a long time coming. I love my wife, but I'm not in love with her. I stayed with her for our children's sake, so it's best she found out. I just wish she had found out in a better way. She left on the rental boat she came on." Looking at her, he realized this woman should have been his wife. He knew about her occupation, but he also knew what kind of woman she was. He wanted to make her an honest woman, but he had to get himself together, get divorced, and GET A JOB.

After another session, they showered, dressed, and headed back to shore, with Mason at the wheel. They would say goodbye at the pier and somehow Lindy felt she would never see him again. He walked her over to Naomi and placed her bag in the back seat. "Lindy, I would like to kiss you one last time before you go, is that okay?"

"Of course." Again, they kissed and he knew he could never let her go. No woman had ever excited him this way, and he wasn't willing to give her up. Holding her tightly he held her face in his hands, "Lindy, I have to see you next week, but the boat is off limits right now. I have to go home and try to resolve this situation. I don't know what's going to happen, but my main concern is not hurting her or my children. I don't want to prolong this anymore. I love you and I will definitely call you." He kissed her again and walked away. After a few feet, he turned back, grabbed her, and initiated another session in the back seat of Naomi. Afterwards, he kissed her again, and walked away.

(Earlier) Ba'Mynn was still in shock, when she

arrived back on the pier and stumbled out of the rental boat. "Lady are you okay? Hey, Lady are you okay?" Bari, the rental boat driver was confused about why she left so fast. He had seen the boat leave last evening with a beautiful woman at the helm and finally understood.

She nodded at the driver and walked toward her car. She had trusted and loved Mason her entire adult life and he had used and abused her. Driving home, her mind set into motion. "First, I will pack up the children and we will leave. Then she stopped, No! He's getting out of my house. I'm the one paying for it. Yes, he hustles and brings home hush mouth money, but it's only when I threaten to evict him. I've had it! Picking up her phone, she called her sister, Kai. Listening to the phone ring, she wondered how she would proceed.

Kai sat in her law office in metropolitan Los Angeles, and picked up her phone, "Hi, Ba'Mynn, I was just thinking that I should call my big sis, what's up?"

Crying and gulping, Ba'Mynn regained her composure and spoke, "Kai, I caught him I finally caught him, and I'm ready to walk away. I was just trying to surprise him, but I got the surprise. He's been spending time out on the water with this woman, and we never left the pier. Prior to catching him today with some woman, I have followed him on several occasions, and watched as he drove out into the bay. He always boarded alone. She must've been onboard prior to his getting there. I hired a driver and went out to surprise him. I walked in and they were in the shower together. He has been carrying on with this woman, while I've been taking care of him.

I've provided him money to run the household, but I always wondered why he needed so much. I lost my relationship with my parents because of him, and I never got it back. She died Kai, mama died thinking I didn't love her, but I did. I forgave her for kicking me out, because I knew she was right. I didn't want to cause her any more pain and set a bad example for you and Blair. I lost everything, everybody, and he did this to me. He's gone and I mean it this time." Ba'Mynn finally broke down.

On the pier, Mason and Lindy had both assumed they were alone, but watching from the boat shack was the rental boat driver, Bari. He had witnessed the entire encounter and thought, "Man, I wish she would do to me what she did to him," as he caressed his rise. Bari wondered if he should go over and help her out, she looked to be crying with her head leaning on the steering wheel of her Range Rover. And! What a nice and roomy Rover it was. Maybe, just maybe he could soothe himself. After all, she hurt the poor woman he took out in his boat, and should be taught a lesson.

Lindy sat in the driver seat and for the first time in years, she had real feelings. And on that note, she cried hysterically. Acknowledging that she wouldn't see Mason again, Lindy pulled herself together and prepared to drive home. Sadly and before she could close the driver's door, a uniformed man stood inside the door, partially clothed from the waist down, and at eye level.

Today had been an extremely slow day at the arena, and the show the woman and man gave him from the parking lot was more exciting than his wife these days. Parked in the private spot next to the dumpster, Bari watched as she sat in the driver's seat. Thinking aloud, "I wonder how many times people have mated in this spot." Hurriedly, he had walked down to her car to get his reward.

Looking around to make sure they were alone he touched Lindy's hair, "Hi pretty lady, I want you to do to me what you did for him. I know who you are and I know who his wife is. It must've been a very nice evening out there on that there boat." Grabbing her head, he pull her close. Crying softly and realizing what was happening, Lindy tried to fight him but Bari held her steady until she obliged. After she had followed his commands, he took full advantage of her.

Bari cautiously looked around before he continued his assault on Lindy. Pushing her into the Rover, he viciously raped her it seemed for hours, until he collapsed on top of her. Trembling, he stood up and stared at her, "Thank you. Now look tramp! Word to the wise, don't come around her again, and I do appreciate your hospitality." Leaning over he spat on her and smiled. Bari straightened himself up and walked back to the boat shack feeling thoroughly satisfied. As he walked back, he hollered over his shoulder, "Hey! Maybe another time." Back in the office he thought, "If I was working I would've missed out on this." For once, he was thankful to be unemployed.

Crying softly in her Rover, Lindy realized that she had just been raped. Struggling to pull herself together, she started her truck, and drove home. Driving down the road, she continued to cry. Not only was her pride hurt, but she was also in physical pain from the brutal assault. In all the years she worked, she had never encountered anything like this.

Several minutes later, she pulled into the driveway, and slowly exited Naomi. She walked slowly to the door. Opening the door and walking into the entrance, she acknowledged her mother's caregiver and spoke to her mother, "Hi mama, I'm home. It was a long night at work." Trying to walk normal, Lindy walked past Ming and avoided her eyes. Slowly, Lindy walked up to her bedroom and straight into the bathroom. Crying, she ran a tub of hot bath water, and cringed as she climbed in. She sat down, flinched from the pain, and realized she was bleeding into the water. The nasty pervert had raped her, torn her with his clumsiness, and his zipper had ripped her. Crying softly she thought, "I'm going to give it to him one more time, and he will never forget it. Smiling through her tears she thought, "Oh I'm

going to give it to him and he will never forget me."
Lindy scrubbed her skin until it bled. Finally, she
climbed out of the tub, and slowly dressed.

Lindy drove to the urgent care center and was
stitched back together. The on call doctor asked her
if she wanted to file a police report and she had
declined. Arriving back home, she walked into her
mother's bedroom and Ming was waiting for her. She
was sitting up in the bed, "Landrea, are you alright?"
Ming used Landrea instead of Lindy when she was
serious. Lindy was a childhood name her parents
used only when they were home.

Her first instinct was to lie, but for the first time
in a long time, she didn't want to. She told her
mother the whole truth about her occupation and the
rape. She was crying and hiccupping before she
finished. Staring at her mother she added, "I'm sorry,

and I'm through with this life. I just wanted to take care of us, so I did what I knew how to do. I'm going to finish my degree soon, and get an honorable job. The house is paid for, and I have quite a bit of money saved."

Ming motioned for her to come and sit beside her. Still sore, Landrea stiffly crawled upon the bed and placed her head in Ming's lap. Ming sang to her daughter as she stroked her hair. Landrea finally fell asleep, unaware of her mother's tears, and pain.

7 ELISSA, "WATCH, WHAT HAPPENS, LIVE!" •

Patrick sat by the window, and polished his nails with Sally Hansen's *quick dry* clear polish. He looked up at Elissa, and knew he loved her very much, but something was missing. They had been married for over seven years, but it was time for change. He cared for her deeply, but he was just very confused. They had not slept together for over five years, so she had to know he was gay. She never questioned him and she took care of him, as if he was her child. She cooked his food, laundered his clothes, put him through multiple schools, and he still didn't have a job. Patrick acknowledged that now was just not the time for working. "Elissa, what time will you be coming home this evening? Do you want me to cook dinner or shall I wait for you to come back?" Patrick stared at her as she grabbed her purse and keys.

Fuming, Elissa glared at him, "It would make sense for you to cook, because you're not doing anything else. I mean, it's not like you have a job or clock in anywhere. I will be at the office until seven o'clock tonight and I will grab a bite to eat on the way there." Elissa looked at Patrick with tears in her eyes and realized that their marriage had finally come to a head. Sadly, she still loved him very much. However, when she got back, she was evicting Patrick and giving him a thirty days' notice. As she walked out of the door and got in her car she thought, "I've taken care of him long enough. It's time for him to stand on his own two feet. He's overly educated so he should be able to get some kind of job. We have no relationship and we don't even share a bed. He spends all of his time down at that fricking nail shop. What nail shop do you know of with only men working in it? And, get this its call, *"Get Nailed."* Elissa didn't know, but a lot more went on at the nail shop besides manicures.

Driving, Elissa spoke out loud, "Topping that off, his nails look better than mine." She arrived at her office and parked near the back entrance. She hoped to get all of her work finished, before taking a week off. It was taking up a lot of time to stay caught up and she didn't want Priza calling her back in. "I need this time to evict Patrick and get my life in order."

Patrick spent a lot of time at the shop meeting people, and watching others hook up. The rooms in the back accommodated those who couldn't go home or were still in the closet. He had almost made it to the back room, one month after his first visit, but couldn't go through with it. Patrick had stood at the door, when the thought of hurting Elissa was more than he could bare. She was good to him and was still his wife.

Eight months ago, Patrick had walked into the *Get Nailed* nail salon. He had learned about it through a mutual friend and wanted to check it out.

He walked through the door, and there sat the receptionist, the most beautiful woman he had ever seen. At least he thought she was a woman until she spoke in a very deep voice. She greeted him and asked how she could help him. Before he could answer, something sharp had pinched his backside. Reacting immediately, he turned around and defensively cocked his fist. Patrick locked eyes with a very handsome man, and quickly bowed down.

Surprisingly, he was very comfortable and with what

he was seeing. The man introduced himself as Benjie

along with his friend Ryan, "Would you like us to

show you around?"

"Sure, I would like that." Patrick agreed and

thanked them. Patrick signed up, joined his two new

best friends, and walked through the first curtain.

Stepping through the first curtain, he saw five nail

stations with men servicing customers. The

customers were *Round the Way* people (dread locks,

shaved heads, spikes, bald, and more), sipping

sparkling white grape juice in champagne glasses. It

wasn't what he expected, since these people were only

getting manicures, pedicures, and gossiping. He had

expected so much more.

One of the men waved at Benjie, "Hi Benj, who's

your new friend?" Benjie waved back and pulled

Patrick through a second curtain, where a bar and

multiple tables aligned the walls. Now this was more

like it. There were people dancing and drinking

everywhere and there was even karaoke. Patrick

began to relax. Staring, he saw the third curtain,

which wore a member's only sign. Benjie motioned

Patrick to the bar, "We will be back shortly," and he

and Ryan went through the third curtain. He sat and

enjoyed people watching. Everybody was enjoying

themselves and appeared to have no worries. Patrick

jumped! The doorbell interrupted Patrick's thoughts

and he went to greet his guest. Opening the door, in

walked Benjie and Ryan with food and drink.

"Hi guys, I'm glad you could make it." Patrick

greeted the pair and they all settled in to watch,

"Watch What Happens, Live!" This was the first

Sunday they were able to come over to Patrick's condominium, instead of at *Get Nailed*. They all loved to watch the reality talk show host and lusted after him, shamelessly. You see, he was the man they all wanted to be and to be with. To them, he was all that and some extra stuff. He was handsome, intelligent, successful, and he wasn't in the closet. So every Sunday and days in between it was the trio, and their show at *Get Nailed*. Benjie who loved the idea of *dress up*, instructed everyone to *gown up*. "Hey let's put on our uniforms and get ready for the show."

Ryan stood and slipped off his pants, exposing his leather thong with an elephant trunk. Underneath his coat, he had on his favorite "talk show host" shirt. Benjie and Patrick exclaimed! "Nice" and both went to change. Benjie reappeared in a gold one-piece leotard and leopard colored pumps.

Benjie shouted, "We are the stars of this fortress tonight." They were waiting for the host's entrance via the television, and Patrick's entrance. Minutes later, Patrick reentered the television room, with a dark blue suit on, white shirt, a light blue tie, and black Gucci shoes. He had even combed his hair like the show's host.

Benjie and Ryan stared at Patrick with thirst. Finally, Ryan broke the silence and spoke to Patrick, "Pat, you look even better tonight." Un-breaking his gaze, Ryan continued, "Is it truly going to happen tonight? We have waited a long time to connect with you."

Benjie added, "Patrick, if anything this should help you find yourself and maybe some peace." Smiling he added, "You may even decide to get a job. We play, but we still work and support our families."

Staring at them, he remembered how they had tried to engage him, but he had always held them off. Elissa always came to his mind, guilt would take priority, and he couldn't betray her.

Patrick looked at the two of them and laughed, "Let's have some wine first, watch the real host, and go from there." Further diverting the conversation, Pat kept talking, "Look at his eyes, they are so cute. I want surgery so I can get my eyes like his."

Ryan shimmered his eyes, and the trio laughed and kept drinking. A couple of hours passed and they were light as feathers. Fully inebriated, Benjie and Ryan stood on the table and danced as they watched the host. They grabbed at each other and hugged atop of Elissa's new coffee table. Patrick positioned standup posters, of the show's host, around the living room. Grabbing his camera, he took pictures of

Benjie and Ryan dancing, Benjie and Ryan cuddling, and Benjie and Ryan hugging the posters. In turn, they took his pictures.

Patrick looked at his watch and realized that it was almost six thirty. He knew Elissa would be home soon and decided to out himself. He grabbed Benjie and Ryan by the hand and led them toward his bedroom. The three of them had never consummated their relationship, but all agreed they were on the "Down" and should never have gotten married. Most of all, Patrick acknowledged that they were his friends and he didn't care if they were gay or not. They were human beings and welcomed him into their circle. The three fell into Patrick's bed and quickly fell asleep, Patrick with clothes and all.

It was almost eight o'clock when Elissa pulled into the parking garage. She slowly grabbed her purse, dreading what she had to do. Her living situation with Patrick had went on for way too long. She truly loved him, but she thought of him as her child, and sometimes a little brother. One thing was for sure, he had to go so she could get on with her life. She truly wanted children someday and that required a real husband.

Stepping out of the elevator, she walked down the hall to condominium number 1202 B, unlocked the door, and stepped inside. Looking around, she quickly saw her living room was a mess and her new coffee table scratched. At first, Elissa was scared for Patrick's safety, but noticing the three wine glasses, she became enraged! "Patrick! Patrick!" Fearing the worst she grabbed her cell phone and walked toward the bedrooms. She stopped at her office first and found it secure, and slowly she moved toward

Patrick's bedroom. Approaching, she noticed the door was wide open and peered in. Patrick was lying on the bed asleep, in his blue suit, with two half-naked men lying beside him. Elissa gasped! "Patrick! What's going on in here?"

Patrick jumped up in confusion, and startled Benjie and Ryan awake as well. "What! What! Oh! Hi Elissa, I'm sorry we fell asleep. You said you wouldn't be home until seven."

Still in shock, she mumbled, "It's eight o'clock." Elissa kept staring at the elephant trunk, and the leopard shoes or whatever it was.

Benjie and Ryan hurried pass Elissa, but didn't make eye contact. They grabbed their clothes from the living room and hurried out the front door. When they reached the car, Ryan asked Benjie, "Do you think it worked?"

Ryan smiled, "I sure hope so. Pat has been scared to move forward. We did him a favor by helping him get caught. That little pill in his wine set the stage, so now we will wait for his call. I hope she recovers, because she sure is a pretty woman. Latina and strikingly gorgeous. Maybe that's why he has been hanging on to her. He doesn't have sex with her, nor with us, and I know he's still a *backside virgin*. Maybe he's not gay." They got into Benjie's car and drove away.

"Elissa, I'm so sorry. I didn't want you to find out like this, but I've never cheated on you. I quit having sex with you, but I never had sex with anyone else, male or female. I have felt afraid, and indifferent my entire life, but I loved you so I married you." Crying softly, Patrick walked over to Elissa as if waiting for her approval to become the real Patrick.

Elissa quickly hugged him, and then pushed him away, "I have known something was wrong for a long time, but I hoped that you would pull yourself together and be a husband to me. Hanging out at that nail shop with men was a dead giveaway. When I left this evening, you were polishing your nails, and it finally hit me that something was terribly wrong. I came back this evening to tell you that it's time for you to move on with your life. Next time, I want to get married for real, have children, and have a real chance at happiness. Patrick, you have thirty days to move out, whether you work or not is up to you. I have taken care of you long enough and I'm done." Elissa stood firm and waited for a response.

Scared and overwhelmed, Pat pleaded, "Elissa, I don't have a job. I can't afford to live anywhere else.

Get Nailed is a place where gay men go to get lucky. I have been there many times, but I've never had relations with anyone. I have seen many people hooking up, but I never crossed the line. I wasn't turned on by any of it. They are my friends and they accept me with no strings and I accept them for who they are."

Returning to her purpose she responded, "As far as a job, there is always the nail shop, and it's not my concern anymore. You need to start looking for a job so you can go. You mentioned a partnership at the nail shop, if I remember correctly. It doesn't matter, I'm done!"

Patrick looked at Elissa and realized he still loved her. Grabbing her, he tried to kiss her and pulled her to him. Finally, he cuddled her in his arms and began to kiss her with an urgency. Resisting at first, she quickly forgot how she had found him, and returned

his kisses. She had been deprived for so long, it just

came natural. Finally pulling apart, Patrick tore off

his clothes and stood in his birthday suit.

Elissa looked at him, "You have been involved

with men and you said you were unable to become

aroused. Now you want to be with me. I don't know

what to think."

Finally understanding that he loved his wife, he

was able to move past suppressing his feelings.

Patrick walked toward her and raised her dress up

over her head. He tasted her neck and smiled,

"Ohhhh! Elissa, I have never cheated on you with

anybody." She smelled and tasted so sweet to him,

just as she used to. It had been five years and he had

never forgotten her smell. He pulled her to the floor,

rolled over, and reintroduced himself to her. He had

enjoyed her for over an hour, when he finally unloaded five years of loneliness. Patrick shuddered and cried softly. He realized he loved this woman and wanted to fix his marriage. He had never acted on the other feelings, and right now, he had no desire to do so. Lying flat on the floor with the back of his hand over his eyes, he mumbled, "I love you Elissa and I don't want our marriage to end. I will start looking for a job tomorrow and I will take care of you, we will have a life together, I promise."

Choking on her tears, Elissa nodded and decided to enjoy the night for what it was. Fully satisfied with what was happening, she still yearned to have her fire put out. Elissa chose to forget, for the moment. After all, it had been over five years and she didn't want to waste any more time. Patrick remembered how good they had been together and hoped for more times like this. He wanted her to remember this day for the rest of her life.

After resting for a few minutes, Elissa looked in his eyes and began to cry softly. "Why didn't you tell me you preferred men, I would have let you go. You have been so unfair these past years. I have been so empty. I never once discussed how we were living with anyone. When I left today, you were polishing your nails, and for the first time I wondered if you were gay. Please tell me you don't have HIV/AIDS or some other type of disease."

"Elissa, I have never cheated on you. I was hanging out with them trying to find myself. I never once engaged into anything with them or anyone else. We would meet at the nail shop, and I would sit at the bar and watch TV. I never criticized them, and they became my friends. Tonight they came over to watch the reality show, Watch What Happens, Live! I

wanted to surprise them, so I dressed up like the host.

I intended to sleep with them, but I think one of

them put something in my drink. I remembered

going to my room and falling asleep on my bed.

Nothing happened. Nothing has ever happened.

Until today, I didn't know where I was going or what

I was going to do. I polished my nails because I

wanted to see how they would look." Holding his

hands up and pointing at his feet, she saw they were

polish free.

Elissa listened to him and wanted to believe him

so bad, but she couldn't forget the scene she

witnessed in his bedroom. The two of them almost

nude and Patrick fully clothed. Maybe he was telling

the truth, he did have his clothes on.

"Pat, I came home to serve you with eviction

papers and I found you in the bed, in our house, with two men. What do you expect me to think?"

In spite of what she had discovered, she grabbed his hand and they walked back into the living room. Seeing the three wine glasses, she grabbed the bottle on the coffee table and refilled two glasses. "Pat, let's have a drink and talk about what just happened. I'm still in shock from this entire evening." Taking a sip, she suddenly had an idea. Standing, she cleared the coffee table, poured wine over her body and stretched out on the coffee table.

Patrick looked at her, and took a big gulp out of his glass. Kneeling over her, he began to lick the wine from her skin. He over exaggerated touching her body to make her vulnerable. He continued to taste the wine, and suddenly felt heat and heaviness. Patrick understood that he desired her, and gently touched her lips with his fingers. She ravenously

licked his fingers and he returned the favor. He loved

the sweet smell she always had and hoped he would

be invited to stay. Drinking of each other, they fully

took advantage of each other in all ways. After an

hour or so, Elissa lay fully exhausted on top of the

coffee table. Watching her lying on the table, he

acknowledged he loved this woman and he wasn't

gay. They continued throughout the evening with the

same behavior. Because they were love deprived,

they stayed together for most of the night. They

christened almost every room in the house and left

their mark on every piece of furniture they owned.

Finally ending up in their marital bedroom, amongst

the pink ruffles of her bedspread, and prior to

christening their marital bed, they fell asleep.

The next morning, the sun shone through the

curtains and Elissa woke up. Feeling around for Patrick, she realized he was gone. Elissa began to cry, as she understood last night was their goodbye. Getting up she grabbed her robe, and walked to his room. There sat Patrick naked on the side of his bed and he was crying. "Good morning Elissa, I got up so you could get some rest. Did I wake you?"

Elissa hesitated before speaking, "No the sun woke me up. Pat, why did you leave? I mean I thought you had left." Guardedly she asked, "Where do we go from here?"

Reaching toward her, Pat motioned for her to kneel in front of him. Thinking he wanted to talk to her, Elissa obeyed. Grabbing himself, Pat showed her what he was working with. "Elissa, as soon as you walked into this room, I came back to life. I don't want to live without you, and I'm sorry I put you through this mess. I love you and I want to spend the rest of my life making it up to you, if it's not too late."

Wanting to please her, he sat on the floor and nibbled her ears. As he teased her, she started to moan and pulled on his ears. He gently nibbled on her lips. Again, they entertained each other.

In the midst, Elissa stopped because this all felt too good to be true. As she lay in Patrick's arms, she gasped! "Patrick, I'm not on any birth control, because I haven't needed anything for the past five years. If I become pregnant, what will we do? I want children, but I never wanted to be a single parent."

Patrick smiled, "I want you to have my child, no my children." With that said, he got to work, in attempt to love away her emptiness. Time was flying, it was past noon, and they had not eaten or drank anything since the previous evening. Standing they

headed to the kitchen to prepare some food.

8 CONFIDING AND CLARITY ◈

Driving home today, Priza could not help but think about Eirik's two-week deadline. Today was the day for him to move out and he hadn't enrolled into anything. To top that off, he still didn't have a job, and was possibly cheating. Late night phone calls, what did he take her for, a fool? Did he think she was stupid? Driving down her street, Priza recognized her mother-in-law's car parked in the driveway and thought, "Great, this should make it somewhat better, because he has somewhere to go."

In the beginning, Priza had not seen eye to eye with Kate, because Kate hadn't accepted her disability. She distinctly remembered Kate's words the night before the wedding. Priza had left the two of them in the living room, and upon her return, she had overheard Kate asking Eirik, "What kind of wife and mother will she be? She has no legs. Eirik, she's not a whole person. You already have one divorce under your belt, and you have to consider your children as well." Priza had been overwhelmed with hurt, had abruptly walked out of Kate's house, and never looked back. In response, she had married Eirik anyway, because she loved him. Through the years, she'd managed to care for Kate, but she didn't quite love her.

Over the years, Kate had recognized that Priza was the best thing that ever happened to her son, her grandchildren, and tried to make amends. Kate also knew that she was wrong about Priza and had grown to love her, but Priza remained cold and standoffish.

Priza parked the Escalade and placed her head on the steering wheel with tears running down her face. Eirik had left her no choice, but to force him out of their home. I mean, what kind of example was he setting for the children? Priza exited her Escalade, walked into her home, "Yes, her home," and found her husband and his mother sitting on the sofa. Kate was crying softly, and Eirik was flushed as if he had been crying.

Priza stood as tall as she could with her legs strapped in place. Nodding she greeted them, "Hi Kate." She turned toward Eirik, "Eirik where are the kids? What is going on?"

"I sent them next door. They will be spending the night with the Keels and will be back in the morning." Eirik motioned to her, "Priza come and sit with me. We need to talk."

"Eirik, it has been a long day and I would prefer we just get all this over with. It may be better if you leave before the kids come back." Kate cried harder as Priza finished her sentence. Sensing there was more going on here than she realized, Priza asked, "Eirik, what's going on here?"

With swollen eyes, Eirik looked up at her, "Priza, I'm so sorry, but I need to talk to you. Please sit down." Priza sat down next to Eirik. He struggled for the right words and finally spoke, "Priza, two years ago I was diagnosed with colon cancer. I was in shock the first year, so I quit my job and denied I was sick. I asked God to save me. After a while, I began to feel worst and called my doctor back. I was devastated, a new wife and a new life and I had cancer. I have been going back and forth every week for the past year for chemo and radiation treatments.

I didn't want to worry you with the possibility of my dying, and leaving you alone to raise the kids. My mother promised to be here for all of you, and that's what the late night phone calls were about. I withdrew from life, and tried to spend quality time with all of you. I thought I was protecting you, but I realize it wasn't the right thing to do."

Eirik coughed and continued, "I lost your love and respect. Every night, I sat on the phone with my mother, with her insisting I tell you the truth. Being stubborn, I felt you should know that I had a reason for all of this. Silly me!" Eirik looked desperate and broken, "I've destroyed everything."

Priza began to cry and hugged Eirik, "No! I'm so sorry. I have always loved and will always love you. I just prayed you would get it together, so we could move on." Shaking her head she continued to speak, "You should've told me, I'm your wife, and we have a family." Priza continued to cry, hiccupping in between. Though overwhelmed, Kate stood and walked over to comfort Priza.

Eirik continued to speak, "Priza listen to me, until a month ago, my oncologist thought I was in remission, but I collapsed in his office. They ran some test and found that my cancer had returned. I'm at stage four. They have given me about four months to live."

Shocked upon hearing Eirik's declaration, Kate grabbed her chest and screamed! "Eirik, no!" She leaned forward and passed out. Priza screamed! Eirik cried out! "Mom! Oh Please God No!" Eirik hadn't shared this new information with his mother.

Several minutes later and after the 911 call, Kate

was transported to the hospital where they were unable able to revive her. The cause of death was listed as cardiac arrest, but Priza and Eirik knew it was from a broken heart. They pronounced her dead, and Eirik signed consents for her body to be transferred to Bazile's Funeral Home. Eirik and Priza were still in shock, when Kate was memorialized five days later. The stress of the impending death of her only child was more than she could stand. During the funeral, Eirik and Priza cried the entire service, and the children sat stone faced, unsure of how to react to losing their Nanna. Two weeks later, things were slowly returning to their abnormal state. Eirik was quiet most of the time, and continued his treatment with Priza by his side. Priza returned to work, but overwhelmed with her home situation, she had taken family medical leave.

Ba'Mynn's home life was changing rapidly. Her oldest son, Brent, had returned home on break from college. "Mom, you have always put me and the twins first. They are still babies, but it's time I took care of you. Remember you will always have us. I'm going to transfer to a local college, so I can live at home and help you. Dad has never been the man of the house, so it's no great loss. I love him very much, but maybe it's time to let him go."

Ba'Mynn sat and sobbed, for hours. She cried not only for her broken marriage, but also for her broken life. This man had stolen her innocence at a young age, seduced her, impregnated her, and flat out disrespected her. He had treated her like a child and made all of the decisions. She had never made peace with her parents before they died. She looked at Brent, "He didn't deliver on any of his promises. He stole my life," She screamed! "I'M ANGRY! I want my life back."

Krissy took family medical leave and sat by Karl's bedside for two straight weeks. After returning home, she had found his suicide note proclaiming his love for some woman named *Lindy*. In his letter, he stated how Krissy and Hannah had been a mistake, and were a burden. He had written in capital letters, "I LOVE LINDY AND I FEEL ALIVE WHEN I'M WITH HER, BUT SADLY SHE DOESN'T FEEL THE SAME. I'M CHECKING OUT OF THIS HELL HOLE CALLED LIFE. GOODBYE KRISSY AND HANNAH, I WISH YOU BOTH WELL. OH! PLEASE TELL MY SON TO TAKE CARE."

Lindy was seated at the kitchen table reading the newspaper highlights, and read upon Karl's attempted suicide. She realized he had attempted to kill himself right after their last session. Visibly shaking, she promptly removed him from her weekly roster and wished him well. They also posted his suicide letter, and she was deeply grateful they didn't know her real name. Lindy spoke aloud, "Stupid fool, he had to know it was only a business arrangement, what a weak and stupid unemployed man?" Unsettled, and feeling sad, Lindy closed the paper and went to sit with her mother. For once, she was grateful her mother only read the Japanese newspaper, another luxury that Lindy renewed for her, annually.

Elissa sat in her cubicle and smiled. Life had been good for the past six months and she was thankful to have her husband back. Rubbing her swollen tummy, she reflected back over the past six months. As of today, she was exactly five months pregnant and Patrick was teaching at the local community college and loved it. She thought back five months ago, when Patrick took her to lunch. Elissa was late clearing the phones and had only twenty minutes for lunch. Patrick had pulled her into the quiet room bathroom, and placed a bun in her oven. Immediately, she knew she was pregnant, because her toes curled as he released himself. They'd almost been caught when someone entered another stall, but managed to escape without being seen. After he left, Elissa smiled her way through the rest of the afternoon.

The time for the *talk* had come, so Dawn called her daughter's home phone and waited for her to answer. "Hi Belle, its mom. I need you to come over. I'm getting some things together since you are nearing your delivery date. Bence will be here also.

Can you be here in two hours? If not, I can send Bence to pick you up."

Belle stared at the phone and wondered what was going to happen, "Sure mom I'll be there." Belle hung up, and was barely able to stand. Grabbing her purse and keys, she walked to her car.

Sitting on the sofa, Dawn knew it was time to speak with Belle and Bence, since her guilt had gotten the best of her. Bence had been sexing her daughter for over two years and now she was pregnant with his child. "Bence, I have called Belle over here so we can discuss what's going on." Bence met Dawn's eyes and guiltily looked away. "Look at me! I have known what's been going on with the two of you for the past couple of years. Two years ago, in the middle of the night, I watched you leave our bed. I quietly followed, and watched you walk into Belle's bedroom.

173

You stayed the entire night with her. I went back to our bed and cried myself to sleep. If you were wondering, that is why I haven't had sex with you in two years. I hated her for stealing you and I hated you more for allowing it to happen."

Bence looked at her with blazing eyes, "You miserable bitch, you are a miserable and pitiful woman. You are more guiltier than I'm. You allowed me to use your daughter for my sexual needs to save yourself. You just sat there and watched as I violated your teenage daughter. Did you know I called your name every time I was with her? Earlier that day, she came to me, said she had boyfriend problems, and wanted to talk to me. When I arrived, she had other plans."

Grabbing his hair he cried, "Did you know she seduced me? No! I raped that child. She was naked

when I entered her room, and when I tried to leave,
she rushed me. She grabbed me and bit my private
area until I stopped fighting. She threatened to tell
you I raped her if I didn't spend the night. For most
of the night, I gave her what she wanted and I left in
the morning. I wanted to tell you the truth, but I
didn't think you would believe me. The next day, I
prayed she wouldn't say anything and my prayers
were answered. She said good morning and smiled
like the little girl she was, and never told you what
happened. After that, she cornered me every time
you left this house, and after a while, I looked
forward to it. She excited me like nobody else, but I
always felt guilty when I thought about you. I always
wondered why you were so angry with me, so cold."

Pounding on the wall he cried, "I raped her and I
will never forgive myself. You stood by and watched

me rape your child. What nurturing, loving mother would do that? Now she may be pregnant with my child. Dawn, I can't stay married to you, and after tonight I never want to see you again. I'm living in a real live nightmare."

Crying, Dawn stood up, "You are not innocent. You could have stopped it all before it began. If you were on a job instead of lying around my house, this could have been prevented." Dawn walked back to the kitchen with tears streaming down her face.

Because of medical problems, she had not wanted to have sex for a long time. Bence was right; she had pawned her daughter, and made her his victim. Now, Belle was pregnant by Bence and things had to be dealt with. Earlier in the week, Dawn had researched statutory rape for her state and knew they wouldn't be legally accountable, but she knew they were morally accountable. Dawn paused as she heard the doorbell ringing. She waited with abated breath and walked toward the living room. Bence was standing at the door talking to a police officer.

9 𝒯HE RIGHT DECISION ◆

Eirik had passed away peacefully in hospice care two months after his mother's funeral. Everyday, Priza had sat quietly with Niema and Sergio at Eirik's bedside as he struggled to breathe. He was so happy after making up with Priza, but had no desire to carry on with his life, as the pain was unbearable. He told Priza, "I'm so sorry about all of this. I do love you, and I know you will continue to be a great mother to our children, but I'm tired. Tell them I love them, and they were the greatest accomplishments in my life, next to you." Looking upward he declared, "Okay Mom, I see you and I'm coming." After Eirik's declaration, he closed his eyes and took his last breath. Sobbing, Priza gathered the children and left the room.

The days passed slowly for Priza and the children leading upto Eirik's funeral. It was a small service because they didn't have many family members, but it was tasteful and peaceful. Alexandria and LEKO Aeronautics had stood by Priza every step of the way. Priza and the children spent a couple of weeks at Alexandria's home under the watchful eye of Alexandria's mother. They made sure she and the children had everything they needed, and most of all, love and a family. Thinking they had overstayed their welcome, Priza returned home with the children.

Alexandria encouraged Priza to seek counseling for herself and the children, and she had agreed. After a few sessions, Priza saw progress in the children and herself, and decided they would continue with it. She was beginning to make sense of

everything, and was learning how to move forward.
Priza, the professional, carried the guilt of not
realizing Eirik had been sick. She thought, "I was
resentful of his not working, but I'm so thankful he
had the chance to spend it with our children."
Through therapy, she was able to, "Let Go and Let
God." The therapist encouraged her to join a family
support group and enrolled her and the kids.

Ba'Mynn

Finally, Ba'Mynn was feeling better, and found it
was becoming easier as the weeks flew by. After
weeks of not communicating with Mason, Ba'Mynn
had spoken with him about that day on the boat. He
had not denied anything, had apologized profusely,
but professed his love for this woman. He also went
into a partnership with his friend at the arena, and
was sending money to her and the children, regularly.

He felt he owed her so much more, and always sent more than was ordered. He told her he cared about her, but had to move on with his life and she should do the same. Ba'Mynn was cried out, and determined to start her life again. Brent was her rock and she was so thankful he stayed home and went to the local college. Kai, her sister, had returned home with her for a short while, and she had been appreciative of another woman in the house.

Sharing custody with Mason was hard, but Brent always accompanied the twins to ensure they were coping with the new arrangement. Brent and Mason were building a better relationship and the twins were fine. Ba'Mynn was still a very beautiful woman and wanted to get on with her life. After some time, she had met someone, and was happily dating again. And HE WORKED! Funny, but she felt free and so much better.

Krissy

Krissy and Hannah moved in with her parents, and faithfully visited Karl once a month. After all, he was family and Hannah's father. After reading Karl's suicide note, she had been numb and unable to function. Thank goodness for her parents, they helped her and Hannah get on with life. Weeks later, Karl was weaned from the coma and was breathing on his own. Sadly, he was still asleep, and after two full weeks in the hospital, they had transferred him to a local skilled nursing facility for long-term care. Krissy had refused to allow him to come home with home health services. She had steadfast refused and informed them, "No! I will not take care of him and No! I'm not his wife. He's my daughter's father." As far as she was concerned, Karl and their marriage had died on the day he attempted suicide.

The doctor's felt that Karl refused to wake up, because he didn't want to face reality. They often asked Krissy and Hannah to talk to him. Resentfully, Krissy obliged, but only about Hannah. She had no words for him. Krissy returned to work and felt as if her burden had been lifted. She felt more alive than she had in many years, and was looking forward to life.

After a year, she was still making weekly visits, but only for Hannah's sake. Krissy, glad for her days off, and was relaxing at home when the phone rang. Reaching for it she answered, "Hello, yes this is she." The nurse on the other end of the phone informed her that Karl had stop breathing and they were unable to revive him. Thanking her for the call, she looked at Hannah who was now eight years old. Embracing

Hannah, she told her that her dad had moved on to heaven.

Hannah replied, "It's okay, he will be happy now." It was more relief than sorrow, and Hannah barely talked about him anymore. After Karl's death, Krissy faithfully allowed Hannah to spend time with Karl's son, Hamilton. Thankfully, they could all move on.

Elissa

Elissa felt as if her life was turning around. Arriving home, and after Patrick's visit to her office, he had cooked dinner and served her well. Patrick worked his teaching schedule around her schedule, and made monthly visits to Elissa's office to show how dedicated he was to her. Elissa was sincerely grateful, and was weak from their mating, but would not trade it for anything. She finally had a husband and a new baby on the way. As she had gotten heavier, they had found other ways to entertain each other. Patrick insisted she stay comfortable while he poured out his love to her. Life was good, and they couldn't be happier. After two months, they welcomed Ms. Patrice Elissa and Mr. Ellis Patrick. Yes, twins!

Fortunately, Patrick never got the chance to contract with Lindy. They had scheduled an appointment, but Patrick cancelled at the last minute. He professed to Lindy that he preferred men.

Lindy had politely informed him, "I understand you prefer men and I respect that, because I also prefer men. However, I will be by to pick up my $750 and will consider the contract cancelled. $500 for the week and the $250 retainer fee." Lindy had in fact went by, picked up her money, they had shook hands, and she left. Patrick was delighted with her beauty, but still preferred his wife and bid her farewell. He built such a relationship with Elissa that he told her about Lindy, and they had joked and laughed about it. Most of the money Elissa had provided to Patrick for household expenses, was sitting in an account for their twin's education.

Dawn

Dawn was surprised it wasn't Belle at the door, but a police officer. The officer looked around Bence and addressed Dawn, "Good evening, do you have a daughter named Isabella Marchant?" Grabbing her chest, Dawn nodded, "Yes." The officer continued, "She's at the police department and she has charged you her mother and stepfather, Dawn and Bence Garrett, for the rape and sexual assault of a minor, named herself. We need the two of you to come down to the department for questioning."

Bence asked, "Can we drive down in our car?"

The officer disgustingly looked at Bence and replied, "No, and you should let your job know you won't be in tomorrow. At this point, you both are being questioned for the assault on a child with malicious intent." Loathingly, he looked at Dawn, "And you! What kind of a mother?" The officer caught himself and remained silent.

Dawn replied, "I'm so sorry, so so sorry." Looking angrily at Bence and needing something to say, she added, "By the way, my husband doesn't work."

Down at the police station and after reading Dawn her rights, a female officer questioned her,

"Mrs. Garrett before we go on, I want you to know that your daughter is over at County General. She was involved in a head on collision this evening, but she's alive. She, Isabella Marchant, is in and out of consciousness, but she gave a statement accusing your husband of statutory rape and you as his accomplice."

Dawn broke down and cried, "Please take me to Belle, I have to see her because she needs me. I never meant to hurt her. I love her."

The female officer glared at her, "What are you crying for? That child has been crying for over two years. She needed you when your husband was invading her, and stealing her childhood and self

-respect. I could say a lot more, but I won't."

On the other side of the police station, Bence confessed to the entire relationship, but denied it was rape. "We first had sex when she was 17 years old, and yes she's pregnant. I'm not even sure if the baby is mine."

Jumping across the table, the officer barely missed Bence as another officer restrained him. "You miserable piece of crap, that young girl is in the hospital fighting for her life. She was involved in a head on collision, and it's a good chance she may not survive. How does murder sound to you?" The two officers sat down across from Bence.

Bence quickly stood up, "Are you going to arrest me? Because, if not, I would like to go. Please, I have to get there to see about her. Dawn! We have to get to the hospital to see about Belle, she needs us. I need to tell her that I'm sorry. Dawn! Please! We need to get out of here."

The officer stood up and told Bence, "Let's go." They walked to the lobby and joined Dawn and the female officer. Speaking to the female officer, Bence's officer ordered, "Please take these two out of here and over to County General."

Minutes later, they arrived at the hospital, and Dawn and Bence was ushered into Belle's hospital room. The nurse and Dawn's two older children were there and they didn't look happy. Dawn gasped when she saw her daughter and immediately began to cry hysterically. "Please Belle! I'm so sorry I didn't protect you. I love you so much. Please forgive me, Please! Please you have to fight." Dawn stared at Belle's stomach and realized it was much smaller than normal. The nurse led the four of them into the hall and addressed her, "Mrs. Garrett, your daughter is in bad shape, and if she survives the night she may have a chance. The doctor will speak with you shortly."

Several minutes later, the doctor entered to speak with them. "Scratching his head, he glared at all of them. This child has been to hell and is trying to get back. As far as the so-called baby is concerned, there was never a baby. After examining Ms. Marchant, we realized she wasn't pregnant, but had a tumor. While removing the tumor, she bled out. According to her medical records, she was diagnosed around seven months ago and was told she needed surgery, but she refused. Her words to me were, "I had to pay them back." Dawn put her hands to her mouth because she had never went to Belle's medical appointments.

Shifting from one side to the other, the doctor continued, "Tonight was her breaking point, and while driving she lost control of her car. I don't think she wants to live. While here she has been in and out of consciousness talking about the two of you." He looked pointedly at Dawn, "This child has endured pain way beyond her years, and right now she needs to hear her mother say it wasn't her fault, and that you are sorry. Belle admitted she seduced your husband, but she's a child and he should've known better."

Turning toward Bence, he continued, "Mr. Garrett, please stay out of her room, if you go back in, I will have you arrested." The doctor turned and walked out.

Dawn stood up and walked back into Belle's room. Sitting at her bedside, Dawn began to caress her hand and talk to her, "Belle, this is mom. I'm so sorry that all of this happened to you and I promise I will protect you from now on. I was wrong and I admit it, but baby I need you to fight right now and fight hard. I'm done with Bence, and he will never come near you again. Please baby, fight."

Bence sat with Dawn's older children out in the hallway, Rae and Adrian, and refused to make eye contact. He could feel their stares, but avoided their eyes and the hatred. The transport officers, sensing a possible disturbance, had remained at their side. Bence cried to himself, as he was broken, ashamed, and uncomfortable.

Rae stood up and glared at him, before she walked back into Belle's room. Adrian jumped up and faced Bence, "How could you do this to her? You were supposed to be a father figure to her, to all of us. You raped my baby sister! You are an animal and mama is no better. You both are complete monsters. You have been carrying on with Belle for two years in my mother's house, and now she could die. Get the hell outta here! Now!"

Adrian ran toward Bence and grabbed his throat. Choking him with all of his might, he realized the officers were restraining him and he was only choking the air. The female officer turned toward Bence and offered these words, "You heard him get the hell out of here, before I let him go." Bence walked out of the hospital and went back to Dawn's home.

Back in Belle's room, Dawn continued to talk to Belle as Rae looked on. Dawn couldn't bear to look at Rae, too much guilt and too much shame. Suddenly, Belle opened her eyes. She tried to remove her tubes before the nurse calmed her. Then she focused on Dawn. "Mama, what's wrong? Why are you crying? Mama, I'm sorry about Bence. I forgive you and I'm sorry. I just wanted you to pay more attention to me. I'm sorry for what I did. He kept telling me he loved only you and it had to stop, but I threatened him if he didn't do it with me. Mama, I have a tumor and I can't have babies."

Dawn softly shushed Belle and continued to cry, "Belle, none of this is your fault. I'm sorry I didn't protect you. I will take care of you, I promise. Please forgive me, please!" Holding Belle's hand Dawn continued to massage it as she drifted off again. Alarms began to sound around Belle and the nurse ushered them out as the doctor walked in. Dawn and Rae joined Adrian and the officers in the hallway.

Almost an hour later, the doctor walked out and told Dawn that Belle had lost her fight. "We just couldn't stop the bleeding because of the blood supply to the tumors. Choking on his words, "She's gone. I'm so very sorry, Mrs. Garrett." and he walked away.

Dawn collapsed to the floor and screamed, "No! Please, No!" Rae and Adrian held each other and cried. They all continued to cry as they were allowed back into Belle's room to say their final good-byes. The nurse touched Dawn's shoulder, "The doctor has released her body, where would you like it sent." Belle lay very still like the six-year-old Dawn remembered. Dawn managed to choke out the name of the local mortuary. She was still replaying the words, "her body" repeatedly. "She wasn't a body, she was her baby, and her name was Isabella." Dawn collapsed onto the hospital floor. When she woke up, she was in a hospital bed with oxygen on. They kept her overnight for observation and released her the next morning. Gabby came and took her home.

The next few days were a nightmare, Bence was in one part of the house, and Dawn slept in Belle's old room. Bence avoided her like the plague. She was so busy making funeral arrangements that she forgot he was in the house. Five days later, Belle was laid to rest a week shy of her 20th birthday. Rae and Adrian sat separately from their mother during the services, and they never spoke to her again.

Bence continued to stay at Dawn's house, since he had nowhere to go. He was forbidden to attend the funeral and hadn't wanted to. Dawn's coworkers had attended the funeral and supported her throughout the process, but refused to come to her home while Bence was there. Alexandria had questioned her at the *Repast*, "Dawn, why is he still in your home? You have to get rid of him because he has destroyed your family. Your children have disowned you, and your family won't have anything to do with you. Doesn't that mean anything to you?"

Dawn numbly answered, "He's sorry and I'm as guilty as he's. Besides, he doesn't work and has nowhere to go." Alexandria looked at Priza, shook her head and they walked away. Everyone at work was aware of what was happening, and had shunned her.

Still in shock, Dawn spent most days in her cubicle and ate lunch alone. She wasn't sleeping with Bence, but was giving him a place to stay. No charges would be filed against the two of them, but she was consumed with guilt. Alexandria and Priza stopped by occasionally and asked how she was holding up, but never stayed longer than needed. Bence was making plans to return home, he only had to donate blood one more time, and he would have enough money to go. Dawn had lost everything and refused to give him anything, except a place to sleep.

On the morning of Belle's 20th birthday, Dawn was sorting through Belle's old clothes when the doorbell rang. She walked downstairs, but Bence had answered the door. Two immigration officers stood with their identification badges shoved in his face. The first officer spoke, "Mr. Bence Garrett, where are you from? Did you enter this country legally?"

Bence didn't appear to be shocked and answered their questions, "I'm from Europe, and I entered this country illegally." The second officer handcuffed Bence and right before he walked out of the house, he turned toward Dawn, "Happy Birthday Belle. Rest in peace, and I'm so sorry. Good-bye, Dawn." The officers led Bence away. Dawn didn't know, but Bence had called immigration, in an attempt to right some of his wrongs. Dawn stood in the doorway, but was unable to respond. At that moment, she realized she just didn't care.

Alexandria

After Max left her home, he had called her later and asked for his clothing. Alexandria had tied them up in three garbage bags and left them on the front sidewalk. After the physical assault on her and the kids, she'd secured a restraining order, and he wasn't allowed within five hundred feet of his family.

Max wasn't allowed to see the children for another three months, and it would be a two hour supervised visit. Alexandria wasn't receiving any child support since he didn't have a job. Last she heard he was living with the rest of the Artist down near the boardwalk, and she honestly didn't care. She had sold her home, and bought a three bedroom bungalow and was doing quite well. She wasn't interested in dating anytime soon, since the kid's happiness and safety came first. She was also modeling again, but only part time. If she decided to date again, an occupation was mandatory, but in between jobs and nonworking men were not acceptable.

Alexandria was readying the kids for their visit with Max, and she was extremely nervous. The social worker would remain with them the entire visit, along with a guard, to ensure he didn't try anything stupid. Maxie and Sari sat quietly on the couch. Priza had come over for support.

Ring! Ring! Ring! The phone was ringing, Alexandria answered, "Hello, yes this is she." Standing for a while, she listened and finally replied, "No I didn't realize he had moved out of state. I haven't spoken with him in over four months when he picked up his clothes. He doesn't even know where I live. Thank you, I appreciate the call."

Alexandria hung up and turned toward her children,

"Your dad has moved back to Boston so you won't

be seeing him today." Afraid of their response,

Alexandria waited for a reaction. Maxie stood up and

Sari yelled, "Yay! Mommy I didn't want to go."

Maxie let out a sigh of relief, "Neither did I, I

don't ever want to see him again."

Priza and Alexandria hugged the children and

knew they could all relax.

Gabriella

Reese was busying getting everything ready for

Gabby. She would be home soon and he wanted

everything to be perfect. He had gotten the biggest

cake he could find and written on it, "I love you more

than anything in this world. Gabby, Baby! Guess

What! I got my job back at the hospital." He had invited their parents over and a few close friends to help him celebrate his entering the job market. Hearing the sound of her car pulling into the driveway, Reese shouted, "She's here. Everybody take your places" Reese hid in the closet by the entrance, and the rest scattered throughout the home.

Gabby was running a bit late today because she had stopped by the doctor's office to find out if she was actually pregnant. She had used the in-home pregnancy test, and had gotten a "+" twice, but she wanted to be sure. Driving home, she cried, because things were not going well at all. Bringing a baby into this mess was a bad idea and she didn't know how to handle it. Maybe she should move back home with her parents and raise the baby with their support. Maybe she should abort it, goodness knows he or she deserved a better life than what she was living. Topping that off, she was on the verge of losing her fricking job because Reese wanted to rendezvous every morning. Gabby drove onto her street, and decided she was moving out. Moving in with her parents had to be the best thing to do. She really loved Reese, but enough was enough. She needed her job, because she had to take care of her child.

Gabby pulled into the driveway and exited her car. Walking up onto the porch, she rehearsed what she was going to say, "Reese, I can't do this anymore. I'm leaving this weekend and moving back in with my parents. Gabby put the key into the lock and walked in. Opening the closet to hang her jacket, Reese jumped out and screamed, "Surprise!"

After being scared nearly half to death, Gabby looked at him, and asked, "Surprise about what?

What have you been doing all day?" Reese grabbed her hand and led her toward the kitchen. Reluctantly she allowed him to lead her, "Reese we have to talk."

Reese led her through the kitchen door and their parents and friends screamed, "Surprise!" Puzzled by what she was seeing, Gabby walked to the table, and read the cake, "Gabby, I love you more than anything in the world. Baby! Guess What! I got my job back at the hospital." Gabby held her hands to her face and began to cry. No blood tears anymore, but tears of joy.

"Why are you crying? I thought you would be happy." Reese hugged her and looked at their family and friends. Facing her, "Gabby, I thought you would be happy. They offered me my position back with the same salary, and I start Monday. Baby we can start over and do all of the things we talked about."

Finally able to speak, Gabby smiled, "I'm very happy, but it's not just the two of us anymore. In seven months, it will be the three of us. Reese I'm pregnant."

Hugging her tightly, he kissed her and added, "I love you, and I will work very hard to make you happy and take care of you and our baby. I love you so much and I thank you for supporting me through all of this. I promise to fulfill all of your dreams, starting here and starting now." Gabby embraced Reese and started to kiss him, while everyone cheered them on. Gabby's dreams were finally coming true.

Priza finally went through Eirik's personal belongings and donated most of it to charity. While cleaning out his drawers, she had found a card with

Dr. Landrea aka Lindy, unlicensed sex and marriage therapist. She had just learned about this woman from Ba'Mynn, and had researched and read about her. Dr. Landrea was in town for a seminar. She wondered if Eirik had received entertainment from her. In another drawer, she also found a savings book, noting that most of the money she'd given him was in the account. He had saved it to protect them. She had cried softly and thanked him. "I love you Eirik, rest in peace."

The next morning at LEKO Aeronautics, Priza made an announcement at the nine o'clock manager meeting. She'd read about the infamous Dr. Landrea Hartford aka Lindy, former sex and marriage therapist. I would like all of the managers and supervisors to attend, and some of the employees. In light of the personal issues affecting our staff and work productivity, we have to be better prepared to assist our employees. I have the sign up forms and the company will sponsor us.

Lish was the first to speak, "Aren't you being a bit presumptuous?"

Priza answered quickly, "It's not meant to come off like that, but this year has been challenging for a lot of us. I would like everyone, if interested, to attend."

10 Lindy, "UNLICENSED, SEX AND MARRIAGE THERAPIST" •

The seminar would begin soon, the auditorium was packed, and all eleven hundred seats were booked to capacity. Lindy was backstage with her husband preparing to go onstage. Although she had facilitated these seminars for many years, she always got nervous right before she stepped onto the platform. Her husband kissed her and took his seat in the preferred section of the auditorium.

Dr. Lindy began, "Welcome ladies! I just want you to know that ***The Struggle Is Real!*** Your husbands don't work because they are busy with Lindy! Your husbands don't work because you enabled them, by taking care of them. My name is

Dr. Landrea Hartford, but for the sake of this conference please call me Dr. Lindy. I want to welcome you to the seminar, **Why Won't My Husband Work.** In addition, there will be a book signing directly after this session. There will be books available for purchase, and I will sign those who already have their books." The audience stood and welcomed Dr. Lindy. Clapping sounded throughout the auditorium.

"Ladies! Again, I want you to know that the Struggle Is Real! Can you all repeat after me? The Struggle Is Real!" The audience chimed in, "The Struggle Is Real! The Struggle Is Real!" for several minutes. Satisfied with their participation, Dr. Landrea addressed the audience, "Some of you have encountered me in one way or another, because I have entertained some of your husbands under the same pretenses, but under a different name and via a different person. I haven't physically met any of your husbands, but I assure you that there is a Lindy in every city, on every street, and in every neighborhood. Because of my unforgettable past, in which I'm not proud, I have sponsored these seminars for over ten years. This is my way of righting some of the wrongs that I injected into other people's lives."

Dr. Lindy began, "Women who live with men who refuses to work needs special attention and guidance to determine the best way to put their lives back on the right track. These women need to move on or find ways to put their spouses back to work. Some of them will move on with their lives, but some of them will choose to stay. For whatever reasons, the decision is theirs and theirs alone. You see, for many years I made my living off women who worked very hard and took care of their households. Although, I have worked as a sex and marriage therapist for many years, many women out there have filled this same position. By becoming Lindy, they provided the love and support your significant other felt they were missing from you. After receiving therapy, many husbands stayed home, and became employed and responsible husbands."

Taking a sip of water, Lindy continued, "You see, I fed them, soothed them, rodeo roped them, and pleasured them. I encouraged them, and most importantly, I LISTENED to them. I listened to their insecurities, their hopes, their dreams, and I encouraged them. When I finished with them, I advised them to stay home and become responsible husbands and fathers. Besides who else would take care of them."

She continued, "Realistically, some of these men were in it for their own selfish reasons, mainly sex. Another thing, why would you provide a nonworking spouse an allowance to run the household, when you are the one maintaining the household? Those household allowances were my salaries. You have to stand up for yourselves and you have to stand firm! I worked in the industry for almost twenty years and I'm not proud of it. Nevertheless, I'm reformed and on my way to becoming a billionaire. Not from being a whore, but from being a therapist. Again, I'm not proud of what I did and that is why I'm here to prevent you from wasting any more of your life. I see there are a few men in the audience, and I offer words of encouragement to you as well. But before I go any further, I have a story to tell you."

Lindy started with her relationship with Mason,

being raped, and explained how she got her revenge

from the "rental boat rapist." Lindy began her story,

"It had been over a month since the unfortunate

incident with the rental boat driver. He raped me

when I was at my worst. Not only did he rape me, he

physically injured my body and spat me. He treated

me like trash, and for the first time in my life, I felt

like trash. Because of what he did, I couldn't work

for quite a while, which was my turning point."

Lindy took a breath, "I had spent a beautiful

evening with the one man I would've loved to have as

my husband, but he was already married. We were

out on his boat, and his wife rented a boat with a

driver, and caught us. She boarded his boat and there

we were. She left without a word. We later returned

to shore, pleasured ourselves for the last time, and he

left me. I sat in my Range Rover, Naomi, and cried

unaware that the rapist was watching me. He just walked up, stood inside my door, and forced me to pleasure him. Regardless of my occupation, it was the most horrific experience I had ever had in my life. Then he forced himself on me. I had never encountered this behavior before and from someone so horrible and colossal." Sounds of snickers followed by disgust sounded throughout the auditorium.

Finally, able to quieten everyone, Lindy continued. "Honestly, I'm not trying to be funny. Normally, I would prepare myself if someone was overly endowed. But since he raped me, I wasn't given the opportunity. After that incident, I gave up my occupation and finished my doctorate degree. Anyway, four weeks after the rape and after I was healed, I went back to the arena. I watched him until

I knew he'd be at work, and would be alone. I could've called the police, but I didn't want to cause unnecessary pain. I'm not proud of it, but I was very revengeful. I sat, watched, and thought about how all of this happened because of some trifling ass non-working man. I always blamed myself, because being raped was a chance you took in this line of work. For the sake of it being said, I had to have sixteen sutures to heal from his invasion. I vowed this would be my first and last rape."

Lindy took another sip of water. "After planning and plotting, I picked my date and I arrived at the arena on a Tuesday morning around seven o'clock. I knew he worked until six o'clock that evening. I also knew a woman and a boy visited daily around nine o'clock in the morning. I hate to say this, but I went as a vengeful person. I took my 'A' game and I dressed the part. I knew traffic was slow during this time, so I wasn't worried about being caught. I climbed the stairs and knocked on the rental boat office door."

Lindy motioned knocking on the door. "Knock! Knock! I was beginning to get nervous, but I stood my ground. I knocked again, but much harder this time." Knock! Knock! "Finally, the door opened and there stood my rapist. I clutched my bag closer to my body, felt the curvature of my Derringer, and my confidence returned."

"Hey lady we don't open until nine this morning. You will have to come back later."

Knowing he didn't recognize her, Lindy stepped forward and held out her hand, "Hi I'm Elle and I don't know if you remember me, but you invited yourself into my body a few weeks ago and I wanted to thank you." Lindy flung open her coat and pushed him aside. Her cologne said *Donatella* and her allure said she was willing.

Pausing slightly with recognition, he smiled and invited her in. In his haste, he forgot his wife and son would arrive shortly. "Hi, I'm Bari," As she walked past he swatted her backside. Stepping inside the door, she noticed a sofa bed, walked over, and sat on the edge of it. "I sat so he would know my intentions. Bari, liking what he was seeing, walked over, and tried to force himself on me."

"No, not like this." I sat up and shook my head. Feeling sick and disgusted, I almost stopped, but knew I had to go through with it. I had to get my power back."

Lindy continued her story. Smiling wickedly Bari remarked, "Don't get scared now, because I'm going to give you what you came here for."

Glancing at her watch, Lindy swallowed and tried to prolong it until his wife arrived. Removing her raincoat, she gently teased. Lindy ordered him to sit against the headboard. If he hadn't raped and spat on her, things could've been different. Sitting on the side of the bed, she built up her courage and asked him, "Why did you rape me?"

Bari stared at her, came back to his senses, and tried to get up. Lindy straddled him and pushed him down. Mumbling, "You raped me now you owe me."

Bari came back to his senses and muttered sarcastically, "It was just an opportunity, nothing more. I apologize for hurting you; now let's get on with this."

Finally, thankful to hear the door opening, she realized it was nine o'clock, the moment she had been waiting for. Totally, under her spell, she took him home as he was out of control. Suddenly, the door flung open and their stood the woman and the boy. At the same moment, Bari screamed, "I'M THERE; I'M THERE, NOW PLEASE!" At that moment, Lindy realized what a pitiful individual he was.

Weak, Bari managed to get up, and Lindy flinched as he pulled away from her body. "Honey, it's not what you think. This tramp tricked me, and then raped me."

Standing up, Lindy threw on her raincoat. She addressed Bari, "this is payback for raping me and spitting in my face." Looking at the woman, Lindy said, "Sorry but your husband is a rapist and you deserve to know exactly what kind of man he is. He raped me in this parking lot four weeks ago, and I had to get medical care from his assault. Although he meddled in my private affairs, I chose not to have him arrested. I just wanted you to know what you are working with. If he comes near me again, I will kill him." Walking over to Bari, "Payback is great, but this experience is a lesson learned." Lindy spat in his face and walked out the door.

A woman in the audience raised her hand, "Excuse me but aren't you just a whore? I mean, why go back, and rendezvous with the person who raped you? That's sick and doesn't make sense." Priza's comment was followed by an awkward silence.

Although irritated by the comment, Lindy remained serene, "I was never just a whore, I was an unlicensed therapist, and I had regular clients. I was raped by someone I didn't consent to having sex with. I went back because I wanted to right a wrong. I didn't report him, but he needed to be held accountable for what he did to me."

Lindy looked at Mason for encouragement (Mason nodded), "I provided a service, and they paid me. I wrote this book because I wanted to save women like you from heartache and try to save your marriages. You see your husbands want all that I do to them, but they want it done by you. Please listen to the rest of my story."

Having changed her life, Lindy believed that Mason really loved Ba'Mynn and possibly her too. Out of all her contracts and relationships, she knew that she had to speak with Ba'Mynn and make everything right for the sake of Mya and Myles.

Picking up the phone, she dialed the operator provided number and called Mason's wife.

"Hello." Ba'Mynn was busy making dinner for the twins. "Hello." Still no response, she was prepared to hang up, when she heard her name.

Nervous and almost hanging up, Lindy said, "Hello, Ba'Mynn. My name is Lindy and I'm the woman that was on the boat with Mason. I want to say, I'm sorry and wondered if we could meet and talk. I never meant to hurt you and I know Mason loves you and the kids very much. It was just a contract, nothing more. I'm an unlicensed sex and marriage therapist and I was only trying to help." Silence followed a click. Ba'Mynn had hung up on her and Lindy wanted to call her right back, but waited a few minutes. After all, she was only trying to help, but who Ba'Mynn or herself? "I dialed the phone again and waited for her to answer."

The phone continued to ring. Ba'Mynn stared at it and thought, "The nerve of this woman calling me. She has been carrying on with Mason for a long time. She has nerves calling me." Finally, Ba'Mynn picked up the phone and unloaded on her, "Look, you have already helped yourself to my husband, destroyed our home, and I will never live with him again. Don't bring your guilt and shame to me. ERASE MY NUMBER! If you ever call me again, I will get a restraining order," and she'd hung up.

"I didn't call her again, because I deserved everything she said and a lot more." Lindy continued her story, "Two hours later, Mason called me and asked if he could see me." Feeling pressure in my throat I asked, "Where would you like to meet? Mason wanted to meet at the boat arena as usual. I hesitated because of the rape and our last meeting."

Sensing my hesitation, Mason spoke to reassure me, "I know what happened to you, and I'm sorry I wasn't there to protect you. I also know about the call to Ba'Mynn, not a good move, but it's okay. Meet me Lindy, please!"

"Reluctantly and against my better judgment I agreed. Reaching into my dresser, I pulled out my Derringer, and put it in my purse. You see there wasn't going to be anymore raping. I dressed, drove to the arena, and waited in the parking area.

A half hour later, I was still in Naomi waiting for Mason to arrive. After waiting an additional thirty minutes, I had decided to go home, when Mason walked up pushing a man in a wheelchair. I looked at the pitiful man and realized it was Bari, my rapist. I reached for her purse and pulled it close."

Mason looked at me reassuringly, "Hi Lindy, sorry I'm late. I'm sure you know who this is. I brought him here because he has something to say to you. I was contacted by Bari, when I moved onto my boat and he told me everything he did to you." I looked past Mason and straight into Bari's eyes.

"Ms. Lindy, I just want to say I'm very sorry for what I did to you. I'm not that person anymore. What I did to you was wrong. That last day I saw you, my wife had left me. You see, I was living in the rental office because I couldn't keep a job. After my wife evicted me, a friend, the co-owner of this boat arena allowed me to stay if I would help with his business. That day I took advantage of you has stayed on my mind, and I'm truly sorry."

Bari turned from her stare but continued to speak, "When you appeared at the office, I thought I was being relieved of my guilt. However, when I saw you standing there half-naked it made everything seem all right. Anyway, after you left, I followed my wife and son. I got in my car and chased after them, but I ran out of gas in the middle of the streets and was in a terrible car crash. I've been paralyzed from the waist down ever since. I'm so sorry, and I ask for your forgiveness. If I had not assaulted you, I would be home with my family. But, because I didn't want to work, I was living here. I saw Mr. Mason here, and I explained to him what happened the day he left you. Let me tell you he beat the hell out of me, and the wheelchair. The next day he came back, I apologized again, and here we are." I noticed the bruises and swelling in his face, and began to cry.

Mason motioned to Bari and he rolled back over to the office. I was crying softly and somehow felt free from the brutal attack and the shame. No more blood shed tears. The scars were healed, but my heart had continued to bleed.

Mason walked up and embraced me. "I'm sorry for what happened to you and I will never forgive myself. I would like to spend the rest of my life making it up to you. I have missed you and I love you. I know what your occupation is, but I'm hoping you will resign and become my wife. We have filed for divorce."

I tried to interject but Mason shushed me, "I work now and not for THE MAN, I'm part owner of the arena here. I invested with the owner, and we have started a tour business, we've leased several of the stored boats. I'm happy now, but something is missing." He looked into my eyes, "It's you! When I'm with you, I am complete. No regrets just completeness. When I got this job, you were the first person I thought of."

Mason continued, "Ba'Mynn has moved on with her life, and I support her and my children mentally and financially. We were so young back then, and realized our love died with our youth. Landrea, I love you." Dropping to one knee, Mason opened up a ring box and asked, "Landrea, I've waited for you my entire life and I want to take care of you and love away all of your pain. Will you marry me?"

Lindy stood at the podium with tears in her eyes, "For the first time in a long time, I began to laugh and cry, but for very different reasons."

I continued, "I have to come clean. Mason, I

called Ba'Mynn because I wanted to apologize to her for what I did, but she hung up. I wanted her to know how I felt about you. I've provided therapy to many men, but I connected to you. We understood each other, and I fell in love. Yes, I love you, and I will marry you. Mason, I still want Ba'Mynn to know how sorry I am, please."

Mason laughed at me, "Landrea, no more Lindy. Ba'Mynn has moved on with her life. It's best to leave it alone right now. The kids are happy, and my oldest son is home, going to college locally. I see them every other weekend, and some weekdays. Ba'Mynn spends her time with Harold, and he's a good man. I've met him because he's around my kids. Enough about them, it's about us right now. I haven't seen you in a long time and I need to hold you and love you, please."

I looked around to see if Bari was watching, "Is it safe? I mean, here!"

Mason smiled, "Landrea, I want you, but not in a car." He grabbed my hand, and we walked toward his boat.

Lindy took another sip of water and wiped her forehead, "Six months later, Mason and Ba'Mynn were officially divorced and a month later Mason married Dr. Landrea Hartford, his Lindy. My mother fell in love with him, because he loves me and I have a good and respectable life now."

With tears in her eyes, Lindy addressed the audience, "My word to you, if you don't take care of your home, someone else will. If your husband isn't working, then he's probably spending time with me. If he's not working when you meet him, chances are he won't work when you marry him. Sometimes you just have to let go. Remember, whomever you marry is who you will have to live with for the rest of your life. You can't change anyone into someone else. People are who they inspire to be, you can't change that. Don't provide them money to manage the household. If you are working, then you should be managing your own money. What man do you know handles the household expenses? If they keep the akids, and you don't want daycare, then they should work when you are home. Save yourself some grief, by doing your homework. Make sure he's working before you marry him. May sure he has worked a long time before meeting you. Get to know him truthfully, talk to his friends and family, and make the right decision. Either they have what you are searching for or they are not the right person for you.

232

Remember this could be your husband. Meet my husband and former client, Mr. Mason Hartford. Thank you all for coming."

Sitting in the audience, Mason stood up and applauded his wife. Following suit, the audience stood and began to show gratitude and appreciation for this very insightful seminar and for Dr. Landrea Hartford.

Why Won't My Husband Work?

Work?

The Struggle is Real!

The End!

ABOUT THE AUTHOR

Tori T. started writing novels about three years ago,

 and this is her first published novel. This book came out of fun and confessions and she sincerely hope you enjoy it. She has been a healthcare professional for almost twenty years, works as a community college instructor, and currently resides in Southern California.